MELTING STEELE

Aaron Patterson

StoneHouse Ink 2014
StoneHouse Ink
Boise, ID 83713
http://www.stonehouseink.net

First eBook Edition: 2014
ISBN: 978-1-62482-114-1

The characters and events portrayed in this book are fictitious. Any similarity to a real person, living or dead, is coincidental and not intended by the author.
Melting Steele: a novel by Aaron Patterson

Cover design by © Cory Clubb
Layout design by Ross Burck – rossburck@gmail.com

Creative Edit by Ellie Ann

Published in the United States of America
StoneHouse Ink

ACCLAIM FOR AARON PATTERSON

"I would recommend this book to anyone who likes **James Patterson** or books like his. I can't wait for the next book to come out."

—Sandra Labella, Amazon reviewer

". . . I think if **Tom Clancy** crossed genres, it would look something like this. Well done."

—Roy Bartle

"Looking for the perfect last minute gift for the avid reader on your list? . . . I suggest BREAKING STEELE—fast paced and one of the best books I've read this year. So pleased that this is going to be a series . . . the writing is terrific and the characters come to life. After reading BREAKING STEELE, go back to the author page and grab EVERYTHING he's written . . . you won't be sorry."

—M.J. Weineburg

Also by Aaron Patterson

Sweet Dreams (Book 1)

Dream On (Book 2)

In Your Dreams (Book 3)

Breaking Steele

Twisting Steele

Melting Steele

Airel (Book 1)

Airel (Book 2)

Michael (Book 3)

Michael (Book 4)

Uriel (Book 5)

Uriel (Book 6)

N19eteen (Digital Short)

The Craigslist Killer (Digital Short)

Zombie High (Digital Short)

Elena's Secret: A Vampire Diaries story

For Klayton—you're a little monster, but I love ya.

MELTING
STEELE

Good and evil press together, fighting each other, only to melt into something stronger than steel.

CHAPTER 1

HOTAH SQUEEZED HIS EYES shut and tried to ignore the sounds coming from the next room. He hugged his bear and hid his face in its soft fur. But try as he might, his being was focused on his grandmother.

It sounded like a muffled scream, as if she was being held down. The thin walls didn't do much to conceal what was going on just past his bedroom, and yet the noise was muted.

"Don't you dare, whore. One sound and I'll tear your tongue out. I like my women quiet."

A muted whimper made its way to him. His grandmother was in pain and he knew what it sounded like, what it smelled like, and what it felt like.

Hotah covered his ears and rocked back and forth on the floor. "It's okay, it's okay, it's okay," he whispered. Even through his hands he could hear her crying, his grandfather hitting her over and over again like some kind of drum. It had a sick rhythm to it, as if he was playing an instrument and her pain was the music.

Pressing his temples, Hotah groaned.

His grandfather raised his voice. "Why do you treat me this way? Why do you make me have to punish you?"

His grandmother didn't answer—she never answered. Hotah wanted his grandfather just to end it, to kill her and be done. But he didn't. Why didn't he just do it? Maybe Hotah should. Maybe he could show him what it meant to finish things off.

A hollow thud made his bedroom wall shake. Now he was throwing her.

Hotah opened his eyes and picked up the hunting knife his uncle had given him for Christmas from where it lay by his left foot.

"It's okay," he told himself. Catching his reflection in the blade, Hotah stood, barefoot, and gripped the hilt so hard his knuckles turned white. He smelled weed and sweat and heard the music of fists. A small smile lifted the corner of his mouth.

Holding up his right hand, Hotah dug the knife into his palm. It cut through the skin. A rivulet of blood ran down his wrist. He grunted and cut a second line across, making an X. He imagined making the same mark on his grandmother's forehead. That would make her sing.

IT WAS SUNDAY MORNING, and I was the closest I'd been to a church in a decade. Mandy and I sat in a rental car across the street from the Indian Hills Community Church in Lincoln, Nebraska.

Mandy sipped loudly on her chi latte, studying each person who entered. I tried to calm the butterflies in my stomach. We were here to face Eddie Lofton. Two weeks ago I'd have said it would be a congenial encounter, but that was before we found out he'd hired a hit on his wife.

"What do you think he'll do?"

The more important question running through my mind was, what was I going to do? I recited the list of events that happen when you deal with murderers. "He'll lie and tell us it was all Williams, Inc. We'll keep pushing him and he'll threaten us and when that doesn't work, he'll try blackmail—or something worse."

Mandy looked at me, eyes wide. "You mean he'll try to steal my Yankees baseball card collection? Or—" She gasped. "Make me listen to the latest tween pop star?"

"Something like that."

"Dang, seems like you've got high hopes for this little outing. You know, he could confess and make our job easier. It happens on CSI: Miami all the time."

"Nothing wraps up in forty-two minutes like it does on TV. Eddie Lofton has way too much on the line—he didn't have his wife killed and go through all that he did just to get caught by the likes of us." I drummed my fingers on the armrest, wishing I could be back in my apartment in Boise. Things were simple in Boise.

"The likes of us? Oh, girl, we're like Nancy Drew married the hot Hardy Boy and their twin baby girls grew up to be us."

I turned my head so Mandy could see my full eye roll, but I laughed before I could complete the maneuver. "You're such a dork, Mandy."

"I think the word you're searching for is 'awesome', because I'm ... You know... awesome." She rambled when she was nervous.

"Mmmhmm." I zoned out again, running through the information we had on Lofton, rehearsing the little speech I'd prepared. It would get me in a lot of trouble with him, and possibly get him fired. But I needed to see this out, for all the women who had been killed. They needed justice.

"When does church get out? I think you, Solomon, Rick, and I need to go on a double date when we get back. Rick still hasn't signed off on Solomon yet, and you know they've gotta click if your relationship is going to go to the next level. Oh, and how's Joshua? I miss that guy. Hello?" Mandy asked. "Hey!" She snapped her fingers in front of my face. "You're off in la la land again."

"What? Sorry." I blinked and then focused on her.

She jerked her head toward the church. "When is the last amen?"

I took off my heels and stretched my toes. "I think around noon. You got somewhere to be?"

"Yeah." She pursed her lips, but didn't meet my eyes. I knew she was about to say something I wouldn't like. "I've got to get all cute for our news interview."

"You didn't…" I cursed and shot her a death glare. "I told you just to call Pam." She was a long-time journalist friend who I wanted to give this story too. "This was the only way, Mandy. We have nothing. The only proof is so shaky that a drunk hillbilly lawyer could get it thrown out of court."

"I know. The law is useless here. We have to ruin his reputation. We have proof that he works with Williams, Inc. Once that gets out, there's no way he'll be reelected. And that'll keep the bastard from getting what he had his wife murdered for in the first place. Irony's a bitch."

"Is that what we want?" I bit my lip. There was more, so much more that I wanted to do to this man who had ordered his wife killed. A dark alley, a Bowie knife, and a Dumpster came to mind. Closing my eyes tightly, I took a deep breath. I couldn't let myself think like that.

"Easy, Sarah. This is going to be a huge win for us. For you. He's a big shot and you're taking him down. The press is going to find out one way or the other, so you might as well take advantage of it."

I was so angry, I gripped the armrests until my fingers hurt. A few more words that were definitely not church-approved slipped off my lips. "I'm not getting in front of the camera—I'm only talking to Pam. If you want to be famous, go right on ahead. Without me."

"Oh, chill out." She took a sip of her drink and sighed as if I were the one being pigheaded.

"Mandy, it's not just that," I said. She looked at me with eyebrows raised. "I have to know that you're on my side."

"What? Of course I am."

"No," I said sternly. "I have to know you're on my side."

"I heard you." She leaned forward. "I'm on your side."

"Really?"

"Yes!"

"Than you've got to stop doing things like that. You can't keep going behind my back. You've got to trust me." I took a shaky breath. Having Mandy with me meant everything, but I had to know that she wanted to be there. "With everything."

She touched my arm.

I looked at her intently. "I've got to know I can trust you."

"You can. I swear." She shifted to face me. "I'm sorry. I . . . I shouldn't have called the press. But Sarah, I am in your corner. I'm your best friend."

I sighed and gave her a small smile, then looked out at the front of the church. My heart sped up when the double doors opened and people filed out. It was now or never, and I let myself get angry all over again. Eddie Lofton let his power go to his head. He walked over everyone in his life, including me. And press or no, he was going to pay.

CHAPTER 2

EDDIE LOFTON STOOD TALKING to the pastor at the doorway of the church. And he laughed. How could he stand there laughing at jokes and go on living his life just a few weeks after having his wife murdered? What would everyone say if they knew? Sometimes I wished there was a mark on the faces of murderers, like the one God gave Cain. I'd have one. But still, it'd save a lot of people a ton of grief. And the prisons would probably be a lot fuller—or at least the graveyards.

I marched up the stone steps and Mandy followed. Eddie spotted me and his smile broadened. He was a handsome man, broad shouldered and muscular. It'd helped him win the women's vote. It worked on me in Rio, but it wouldn't work on me this time. "Sarah Steele? Is that really you?" He seemed happy to see me. That wouldn't last.

"Yes, it's me, Mr. Lofton." People stood around, but all I could see was his face. Smug, confident—not at all like the last time I saw him when he was begging me to find the Blondes.

"Mr. Lofton? We're on a first-name basis after all we've been through, don't you think?" He moved forward and gave me a hug. I let him, though I was as stiff as an icicle.

"Eddie, how are you?" I said with as much fake concern as I could muster.

"I'm good. I mean, as good as I can be." Right on cue, his face fell as he took on the role of grieving husband. He took my arm and started walking me down the steps toward the road. I had planned on talking to him alone, but after I saw his face and remembered his wife's body in a Dumpster, I decided differently.

"Cut the crap, Eddie." My voice was hard. He stopped and looked at me, confusion splattered all over his face. I said it just loud enough for everyone within ten feet to hear. "I know you had your wife kidnapped by the Blondes, had her murdered, and sent me on a wild goose chase . . . all the while acting like you were a broken-hearted husband. Tell me, is everything about you a lie, or just the fact that you're in Williams, Inc. back pocket?"

His smile vanished, and fury flashed across his face. Everyone's eyes were on us, and the pastor had out his phone as if he were about to call the police. "Now hold on . . . " Eddie said, holding up a hand.

"No, you hold on. Go ahead—deny it, Eddie. Tell me you had no idea—tell me you didn't pay fifty grand to have her killed. Tell me you had no idea that Williams, Inc. needed her pesky environmental lawsuits out of the way. Go ahead. Tell me more lies, Eddie." My breath was coming in short waves, and Mandy took my arm. It grounded me, and I secretly loved her for it. She knew when to break in, but she also knew when I was on a roll and to keep quiet.

Eddie looked around at all the staring faces and grinned wildly. "Sarah Steele, you're a hoot. I know you like practical jokes, but this is too much." It was a lame attempt at saving face, but it bought him a minute or two.

Lowering his voice, he growled. "You keep this up, and I'll tell

Hannah Williams about you and how you got in the way and almost blew the whole thing."

Anger gripped me and I clenched my fists. "Please, tell Hannah Williams. And give her a message for me." I hit him with a right hook, sending his head twisting to the side. He tripped over his own feet and sprawled face-first on the concrete.

Mandy giggled, clapping and jumping up and down as if we had won a bunny at the fair. I was just pissed. The pastor rushed to Eddie. "I'm calling the police," the pastor stated, then glared up at me. "Leave here at once. This is crazy!"

Eddie stared up at me, his eyes filled with loathing. Blood poured from his nose and the crowd of onlookers stood there with shocked expressions, whispering and pulling out their cell phones. It was strange how in moments of trauma or excitement, it never was like the movies. People didn't scream or run or jump to action. Most of the time they just stood, staring, not able to process what they were seeing.

My knuckle throbbed. It hurt like hell, but the pain felt good. It made me feel alive. At least it wasn't broken, as far as I could tell. "He had it coming."

Eddie cursed, and I heard sirens in the distance. So much for canned speeches and keeping myself in check—now I'd have a lot more to explain to my boss, Dan Butler, when I got back home. If he let me in the door, that is.

Mandy tugged my arm and pointed. A white news van turned the corner and was heading our way at an alarming speed. "News van's here. Showtime, babe. Let's make some media people happy."

As I told the reporters what happened in Rio, I felt a balm over my heart. Although I wished I could do more, it was something. His reputation would be shadowy, at best, from now on.

Eddie ran away, shielding his face from the cameras, and jumped in a waiting car. I hoped I'd never see him again.

CHAPTER 3

HOME.

I was finally back in Boise where the air was clean, the drivers were either geriatrics or Speed Racer, the crime rate was lower than the average American city, and the mountains constantly called at me to be climbed. I loved to travel and needed to get out of town every once in a while, but I also loved being back home in Boise. All I wanted was a shower, to crawl into my bed, and to sleep for a year.

But first I had to get off this tin can of an airplane. We had landed about fifteen minutes ago and were waiting for the doors to open. People shifted in their seats, the air grew stale, and a baby started to cry. Perfect—next thing you know, it would poop in its diaper and smell up the plane before we all got off.

The overhead speaker crackled and a woman's voice sounded. "You may now use all electronic devices, and we will be opening the doors in a moment. Thank you for flying with United Airlines."

"About time," Mandy muttered. "That baby makes me want children in a bad way."

I rolled my eyes and was thankful, not for the first time, that

Mandy and her husband, Rick, had decided not to have children.

She took out her cell phone and began talking to herself and texting. She was probably letting Rick know we were here. I checked mine and saw a text from Solomon. Let me know when you get home. I will be back in a few days. We are wrapping up a case and I miss you like crazy!

My body heat kicked up a little. I ran a hand through my hair. Mandy nudged me, one of her signature dumb grins plastered all over her face.

"What?" I said, annoyed already.

"You like him, I can tell. Whenever you get all hot for him, you play with your hair. It's cute."

"He's okay," I lied.

"Nice try, lover girl. You're so gone for him, and you should be. He's a stud and knows how to keep up with you. God knows I've tried."

I put my phone back in my purse and tried to hide the panic I felt at having a boyfriend. I was a little stressed after all the TV interviews, the mounds of paperwork I had to do for the local authorities, and my voicemail had at least eight messages from Dan Butler. To top it off, I found myself involved in a serious relationship with Solomon, who worked for the FBI and had more secrets than he let on. I knew all about secrets—I had my share, and they made me more aware of other people who were like me.

All I wanted was a vacation, and somehow I even screwed that up and almost got myself killed in the process. I sighed. If I stepped back and examined it, I'd have to say that I wouldn't give up a thing. All the tension kept the darker side of my soul at bay. It kept back the horrible dreams and violent fantasies that had followed me since I was a child. I wished I were normal, whatever that was.

"Come on." Mandy grabbed my arm. "Rick's waiting."

The airport was small and clean, full of familiar faces and small-town friendliness. As soon as we rounded the corner to baggage claim, Mandy squealed.

"Rick." She dropped her purse and ran, flinging herself into his arms. I picked up her purse, shaking my head.

"Babycakes, I missed you so much." They kissed as if the world was about to end, and she wrapped her legs around his waist. The sounds they were making were a mix between an exhausted runner and a dog licking from a water bowl. Ick. I became a little uncomfortable at their public display, but I should've been used to it by now. They'd never been shy about PDA.

"What? No hello for me?" I asked. They ignored me.

"Oh, Rick, you're so going to get it tonight." People gawked as they passed and were secretly jealous, I'm sure. It made me long for Solomon, and the feel of his lips on mine.

I decided to go get the bags and let them finish their exuberant welcome-home ritual.

I couldn't help but be happy for them. It was hard to find true love, and they were one of the only couples I knew who really poured a lot of work into their relationship. I wondered if Solomon and I would ever get there. Did I even want to get there?

Before I knew it, I was home. I made the rounds, checking every room and drawer like a mother hen checks her eggs, making sure nothing was disturbed while I was gone. It was as it should be. I liked to keep my house simple and clean. My décor was so simple that Joshua called me a monk, and Mandy begged me to let her redesign it. But I needed simple—everything else in my life was complicated.

Putting off checking my e-mail just a while longer, I stripped down and slipped into the shower. After a few handfuls of soap, the travel grime was off my skin, but I stayed and relaxed under the sharp jet until my fingers were prunes and my mind felt soggy.

As much as I wanted to slip under the covers after my shower, I had work to do. I logged into my work e-mail and saw five hundred and fifty messages. It was going to take me hours to go through everything.

Vacation was officially over.

CHAPTER 4

HE LIKED TO SIT in his car in the dark and watch. There was nothing all that exciting about an abandoned trailer on the outskirts of town, but it was not what he saw—it was what he remembered. He lit up a smoke and took a long drag. The burn in his lungs felt good.

Much like any killer, a memory brought on by some trophy could be almost as powerful as the event itself—sometimes more powerful. The mind, the imagination, was amazing. He had the ability to recall every detail down to the droplets of blood seeping from around her eyes.

She cried blood. She cried blood for him.

Rolling down the window to clear out the smoke, he panted for a moment before catching his breath. Yellow crime scene tape flapped like a broken arm in the soft breeze coming up from the river.

Was it really a few weeks ago? It felt like he was standing over her just the other day. Time was funny—it was as if he could walk through a thin spot and move in and out of time at will.

Getting out of his dark purple Honda Civic, he shut the door quietly and made his way toward the empty trailer. Everything was dark and quiet except for a dog barking in the distance. All the trailers in this park were far apart, which worked against him. It made it harder to get around unseen, and someone like him could sneak up and surprise him. He laughed—as if anyone could sneak up on him.

What are you doing? You're going to get caught returning to the scene of the crime.

Stopping to consider this, he shook his head and moved closer to the front door. He had to see it again, where he had choked her to death and the spark in her eyes went out. It moved him, and changed him. There was nothing so spiritual as experiencing a soul leaving the body. It was as close to God as a human could ever get.

But it was a thankless business. She cried as he squeezed the life out of her and pissed all over his shoes. Why did she have to go and piss on his shoes?

He touched the end of the yellow crime scene tape and let the memory flood through his mind.

There she was—he saw her in his mind's eye. He smelled her shampoo—her skin and her fear. Muttering, he let the tape fall and reached for the doorknob. As soon as he touched it, his body jerked with pleasure. Like a jolt of electricity, memories of that night ripped through his very core and he went to his knees.

He could see her white neck, the smooth part that connected to her collarbone. This was it, the very moment he'd dreamed about—the part he needed to feel again.

A bulging, panicked look had lit her face and he couldn't help but smile. She knew he was here to kill her. He could see it in her eyes, knowing that this was the end and just who he was. And who had sent him.

Still on his knees, the killer gripped the air and ground his jaw. "Now die."

How could something so hated be so beautiful? This was not murder—it was love. He loved her, loved each one of them—loved them to death.

CHAPTER 5

"STEELE." DAN BUTLER YELLED at me from down the hall. Whenever he used my last name, it meant a butt was about to get chewed, and that butt was going to be mine. I nonchalantly turned the corner, pretending I didn't hear.

"Steele, don't act like you can't hear me."

I turned to face my boss. He was dressed impeccably in a designer suit, with a haircut that was more expensive than my shoe budget, and he would look absolutely charming if I didn't know him for the pretentious ass that he was. He acted as if he was the chief justice of the United States, not the district attorney of Boise.

"Hello, Dan," I said offhandedly. He hated it when I downplayed his anger. I loved what he hated.

"Steele, you're on paid suspension till further notice. Pack what you need and be out by the end of the day!"

I assessed him, reading the danger level on his face. He stared back at me intently. Dang, I wish I had answered my intern's phone calls that morning. This was probably what he was warning me about.

Looking down, I tried to steady my voice. "Why?"

"Because you're a killer," he said flatly. I opened my mouth to say something, but he held up his hand. "You shooting Williams was a disaster, but it was a disaster we could handle because the police were there and you were attacked and it was all self-defense. Easy-peasy to feel sorry for you and the public to go on their merry way." Then he lowered his voice, and it had a hard edge. "But killing two young, beautiful native girls while on vacation? Sarah! Even if they were murderers, it doesn't erase the fact that you killed them. I can't let this go unpunished, or at least without investigation."

I glared and opened my mouth to speak again, but he stuck a finger in my face. He wasn't done.

"Not only that, but you've ignored my calls. I have to see you all over the news and find out about this case you were supposed to be done with from TV. I should be the first person you call. How do you think that makes me look—how that makes this office look?" He ran his fingers through his dark hair in exasperation.

I clenched my jaw, unwilling to say anything I'd regret. I was a lawyer, after all, and knew it would be held against me. But I wasn't going down this way—that much I knew. Taking a deep breath, I gathered my thoughts. The office was quiet. Everyone must be listening.

His eyes softened. "When I hired you, it was out of pity. And because you had a view I didn't have—namely, that of a guttersnipe. I thought the press would love a good Cinderella story, you coming from the foster care system and poor as dirt and working your way through law school. Hell, even your parents' story is so pathetic, no one could help but feel sorry for you." He leaned forward. "But you know Cinderella's magic doesn't last."

Now I knew exactly what to say. "You've told me that a hundred times, and you know what?" I came within an inch of his face. "I'm not Cinderella, I'm not the ugly stepsister, and I'm not the fairy godmother.

This isn't a fairy tale. You don't fire lawyers. You don't fire me. I'm going to come at you with everything I have, and I won't do it in public, either."

He winced, confused.

I whispered, "I will ruin your life from the inside out—I'll show every political friend of yours what you've done behind their backs. Every client you cheated will find out, every dirty little thing you've texted me over the years will come out, and you'll have to account for every law broken and every law you've made us break. When I'm done, even your mother won't work with you, and you can kiss running for mayor good-bye."

He stepped back and laughed without humor. "What is wrong with you? I thought you'd be all relaxed and happy after your vacation." When he said the word "vacation", he made air quotes. "You're getting paid, so what's the big deal? Besides, I can throw you some freelance work, if you want. You know, to keep you in the loop, maybe get back in my good graces."

I swallowed and stepped back, but kept my eyes on him. "What do you want?" I said through clenched teeth.

"I want to hire you, Sarah. This office can't take on every case, and some of these cases could help me—I mean, help us. You could be my girl on the outside and stay the payroll at the same time—you should be thanking me, not acting all hormonal."

I took a shaky breath. My mind was reeling. Something had to change—something was bound to change because of what I did in Rio—but I didn't expect this.

"Just have your stuff cleared out by tonight. I'll tell the press it's only until the internal investigation is over and that you're our pride and joy and other nonsense. Oh, and Joshua's in your office with your first job. A journalist has been calling for you. I want you to help him, no matter what."

"Oh?"

"Yeah."

"Well, you've got one thing wrong." Things had to be on my terms. I had to take this break and run for it. He'd always pushed me around, and in the past I had put up with it because I loved my job so much. But no more.

"What's that?" he asked with an edge on his voice.

"I'm not going to be your girl."

He frowned.

"If I'm going to do this, it's my way. I'll run it under my own business, no under-the-table payments, and it all has to be legit. I'll have a consultation fee and take the jobs I want to take, not the ones you hand out. You pay me half up front—that is, if you can afford me."

I moved toward my office door and glanced in. Joshua, my intern, was in the corner, grinning from ear to ear. Then I turned back to Dan. "I've still got a fully packed suitcase at home, I slept like two hours last night, and I'm greeted back with you yelling at me. Don't say another rash word, and I may think about it."

Dan crossed his arms and considered me before nodding. "Very well, Sarah. I need you on this case. We want this journalist to owe us a favor."

"Okay." I brushed him off.

Dan scowled at me like a disapproving father. "And...?"

I groaned. "And I'll have a resignation on your desk by the end of the day."

"Good." He leaned in as if he was about to tell me a secret. I knew his secrets were never good. "Look, Sarah. I'm sorry I got up in your face right off. It's just that no one's quite as much fun to work with." His eyes flickered to my chest.

I wanted to vomit.

But he didn't let up. This guy didn't have an off button. "I have a reservation at the Arid Club tonight. We could talk about your new business and have a glass of wine. I can help you with it." He saw the look of horror all over my face and backpedaled. "Just business, of course."

I considered punching him in that big nose, but I didn't want to go to jail. "Dan, no. I don't want your wife to get the wrong impression."

"I can keep a secret." He winked, and it took everything in me not to rack him.

"I'm sure you can, but no. I have a boyfriend."

Dan straightened as if I'd just punched him. He huffed right into my face. "I see." His scowl then turned to a smile, and he asked if I at least had any pictures of me and Mandy on the beach. I turned, walked into my office, and slammed the door.

Joshua laughed, and I flipped off the closed door.

"I missed you, boss. No one else treats Dan like that. You can't leave."

My anger melted and I let out a long sigh. "I missed you too." My office was just as sparse as my house, though I did have a statue of blind Lady Justice on my desk and an oil painting of Themis and Astraea, the Greek goddesses who were the personifications of justice. They helped me remember my purpose here and why I took the job with Dan in the first place. "Tell me some good news, Joshua. Something about cute kittens or world peace or that I won a lifetime supply of Godiva chocolate."

He just laughed. "If you want that, you've got the wrong job."

CHAPTER 6

FROM THE FIRST DAY of working together, Joshua and I clicked, and I haven't let him out of my sight since then. He was a tall, rotund, muscular native Hawaiian who had the best taste in music, a quirky style, top-of-the-class smarts, and a beautiful accent. I've proposed to him numerous times, but he keeps telling me that his girlfriend would probably object.

I sat down behind my desk and closed my eyes. "Can you get that number for me, for the reporter Dan mentioned?"

He got on his phone and started tapping. "You've got to see the newspaper on your desk too. It came out yesterday."

I pulled it out from under a file. "Did they finally discover my background as a pirate in Somalia?"

He winked. "Something like that."

My mouth fell open when I saw the headline with a picture of Hank and Glen Williams.

KILLER ADA STRIKES AGAIN

My heart skipped a beat. Surely they didn't—they couldn't have discovered the holes in my story to the police. No one could know that I was the one who set the trap for Williams and not the other way around.

"Yeah, you've been the talk of the building for the last few days. How does it feel to be a young girl's hero?"

What? Hero? I was pissed, scared, and giddy all at the same time. Scanning the page, I took in as much of the story as I could.

One sentence especially stood out to me. Assistant district attorney Sarah Steel is known for her killer instincts in and out of the courtroom. In the last 6 months, she has killed two people in what seems to be a winning streak for the good guys.

The last thing I wanted was for people to know about me or poking around into my past. There were a lot of secrets I wanted to keep in the shadows. First and foremost, the stories of how I killed Hank and the Blondes. My gut clenched. What scared me was that I had no idea if I'd be able to quit. I still had that dark urge, that need for vengeance that was never quiet. I sighed deeply, unclenching my jaw.

"Where are they getting all this? They have some stuff in here that only someone in this office would know." Some of the information was easy to find, like the fact that my mom was in prison for killing my dad. But the paper had mentioned my kickboxing mentorship program, and I didn't talk about that much.

Josh lifted one eyebrow. "I thought the same thing when I first read it. According to the paper, they have a source, but won't disclose it. I wouldn't worry too much about it. Most people think it's cool—you're like a hero. It'll blow over."

"Yeah, right. Just something else to put on my résumé—hero for hire." I snorted. Me being a hero was the furthest thing from reality. More like crazy killer for hire—comes with mental baggage and an overactive sense of justice.

"Maybe you should start your own agency or something—"

"Joshua, come on." I gave him a wry look. "I know you overheard what Dan and I talked about."

"You mean argued about." He grinned at me, making his eyes look like small black dots. "But in all seriousness, if you are going to start an agency, I want in." He stood up. "We can get things done for people who really need it, not these corporate douchebag clients Dan always seems to attract." I held my breath. Was he being serious? The DA's office was his dream job. He continued. "Clients bring us a wrong, and we'll right it. We'll hunt the baddies down, grab the evidence, and make the problem go away." He laughed. I stared at him. After a second, he stopped laughing and blinked at me. "What?"

"Serious?"

"Me? Always."

"You'd really quit this job."

"Come on, Sarah." He sat back down. "You know you wouldn't be able to find your own car in the parking lot if it wasn't for me. How could you run your own company if I wasn't there to bring you coffee?"

He motioned to the steaming cup on my desk and I grabbed it, raising it in a salute. "You're right. I wouldn't dream of going out into the big old scary world without my java . . . er, I mean you."

He went back to his phone, scrolling through pages.

It scared me witless to think about giving up my regular paycheck and backing out of what I always considered my dream job. But dreams change, don't they?

"Okay." He tapped his phone. "Just sent you the contact who's been frantically calling Dan for the past two hours."

My phone buzzed. I opened the text and instantly called the number.

The phone on the other end rang three times and a young man answered. "Hello?"

"Is this Timothy James?"

"Who is this?" His voice took on a higher tone.

"Don't worry, Mr. James. I work with Dan Butler, but he said this had to be unofficial. My name is Sarah Steele." I tapped my pen against the desk. "Now, you've got some trouble, have you?"

"Yes," he said, his voice trembling. "I'm in trouble. And I need you to get me out of it before I end up dead."

CHAPTER 7

JOSHUA SQUEEZED HIMSELF INTO the passenger seat of my car. "An Indian reservation? I didn't know there were any around here."

"There are only a few in Idaho that I know of, and most are small. But I'm definitely not a specialist on Native American law, so I'm not sure what we're getting in to here. And he seemed panicked on the phone."

"Did he tell you why he had to see you today?"

"Nope, just that it was a matter of life and death."

"Same ol', same ol'."

Timothy James was a reporter for NPR and, according to Joshua's iPhone, he had won quite a few awards. He specialized in equality for ethnic minorities and appeared hard-working, driven, and very handsome, judging from the picture Joshua showed me.

The 'burbs and malls and concrete were long behind us, and the mountains, creeks, and beautiful wildflowers rose in front. I felt better each mile we drove out of town. The reservation was 105 miles from Boise, and I was enjoying every one of them. Billboards displayed colorful pictures of blackjack tables, waitresses in short skirts, and luxurious hotel rooms. They even had a Wild Wild West show with real horses and wagons and trick shooters.

"So, how big is the Somneset tribe?" I asked.

Josh stared at his phone. In his big hands, it looked like a kid's toy. "Wikipedia says there are 1400 members as of last year. It looks like they have a bit of a feud going on."

"How so?" I asked.

"There are half a dozen police reports all involving fights. Body count thus far is eight. One involved a standoff at a school after a local election—guess one side thought the other was cheating, and two women in their seventies killed each other."

I gasp. "What?"

"Yeah, I guess one had a heart attack after beating the other to death in her wheelchair."

"You're making that up."

He shook his head solemnly.

I remembered a case a few years back that involved a tribe member—our office couldn't step in without the permission of their council. They were a nation within a nation.

I sighed and relaxed back in my seat. "Timothy wouldn't be dumb enough to get involved in a feud now, would he?" My impression of the NPR reporter was sinking.

"Let's just hope he ran up a gambling debt or something." Joshua pointed to my exit and I took it. The car turned so sharply that Joshua gripped the armrest.

"I have a feeling this is going to get complicated in a hurry," I said.

"No joke."

I pulled into a broken-down café on the side of the road and shut off the engine. The parking lot was full of cracked concrete and potholes half the size of my car. A sign boasted that it had been the home of world-famous chocolate shakes. I saw tables through the dusty windows—some even had plates still on them. This place was trapped in time. The 1960s, from the look of it.

An older car was parked to the side of the building, only its fender peeping out. A man leaned against the back of the car, his arms crossed, staring at us intently. From his body language, I guessed that the big secret he had was hidden in the trunk. I studied the man. He had short blond hair and a rough-cut face with baby-blue eyes. His red polo was wrinkled and splattered with food and his jeans were baggy and limp, as if he'd worn them for a few days in a row. And he could have used a shave and a shower.

"Okay, here we go." I should have been nervous, but I found myself excited. I loved the mystery of it all—the random phone call, a long drive to a creepy dive to meet a stranger over a life-and-death matter. The dark places in my mind stirred, but not in warning—more as if to let me know that here, I was the predator.

"I'll stay in the car, if you don't mind. Depending on what he wants, you may not want me to know."

Josh had a point. He was thinking like a lawyer, and some things could not be unheard. "From first glance, it looks like he's been holed up somewhere. He has that red-eyed, glazed look about him. Keep an eye out and if anything funny happens, come save me."

"What do you want me to do? Cite facts about Hawaiian history until he dies of boredom? Lull him to sleep with a lullaby? 'Cause that's all I got."

I laughed. "You do have the prettiest singing voice." Reaching in front of him, I opened the glove box and took out my gun.

Joshua's eyes turned solemn. "What's that for?"

"It's a gun. You point this end at the bad guy and pull the trigger, and a bullet—"

"Sarah." His voice took on a warning tone.

"I'm not planning on using it. But whenever I'm facing a stranger who weighs twice as much as me, I can't just rely on my kickboxing skills. Now stay sharp."

Stepping out of the car, I tucked the gun in my purse and walked toward Timothy James.

He rushed toward me. Then he looked past me at my car and the huge man sitting in the passenger seat.

"He's my bodyguard," I said, offering my hand.

"Oh, yes. I see." Mr. James was tall, at least six foot three, and lean but fit. I saw panic in his eyes, shiny and raw. But behind that was a deep sadness, marked by the wrinkles around his eyes. "Thanks for meeting me, Miss Steele."

"Sarah." He had my hand in a death grip and I pulled it away.

"Sarah. I'm Timothy—just Timothy. I'm sorry I'm acting like this. I can't put my head in thoughts. I mean, I can't put my thoughts…" He stopped and pressed his lips together.

"We'll deal with this together. First, you have to swear something to me."

His eyes widened. "I didn't do it!"

That was not a good sign—he was defensive, and I hadn't even asked him a question. "I'm not the judge. I'm not the jury. Just promise me you'll tell me the truth, no matter what. I am the one person you do not lie to."

He looked in my eyes for a minute, assessing me. The wind gusted, ruffling his hair. "I promise."

"Okay." I clapped my hands once and pointed to his car. "Now tell me what's going on. And why you wanted Dan Butler on the case."

Timothy nodded nervously and cursed. "Okay, I'm good." He seemed to gather himself and motioned for me to follow him to the back of his SUV. What was in that trunk? I shot Josh a look and he waved at me.

"I see he didn't tell you—Mr. Butler, that is. I requested you, Miss Steele . . . er, Sarah. I've been following your work for a year or so, the cases you work on, your style. I have an eye for talent, for the story that will become a story. It's my job, and I'm the best there is." He said it with confidence, not pride. Just like I'm sure he knew he was good-looking.

"Good for you." I reached for the trunk handle, but he moved in front of it. I folded my arms across my chest. "Now what kind of trouble are you in?"

"Yes, trouble. I'm afraid I'm in the worst kind. I called you because out here, the law is of no use. On the reservation, the law is created by the council. They do what they want. And with your set of skills, I thought you could help me get around the law—or at least, weed through theirs."

"Timothy," I said sharply. "What laws have you broken?"

He grunted, lifted the hatchback, and took a step back so I could see inside. My stomach churned at the sight and smell. I put my hand over my mouth, wincing. No matter how many times I'd seen it, nothing prepares you for the shock of seeing a dead body.

"Yeah, it's just what it looks like." Timothy paled.

Crammed against the back of the rear seat was the twisted body of a girl. Her lifeless eyes stared into nothing, and there was the tail end of an arrow sticking out of her chest. Dried blood caked the front of her dress, and the carpet was soaked with it.

I turned and opened my mouth to say something to Timothy, but nothing came out. He looked at his feet and kicked the dirt.

"Can you help me, Sarah Steele?"

CHAPTER 8

I NARROWED MY WORLD TO this car, this body, this moment. Nothing existed outside of it. There was only so much time, and I had to employ every second to memorizing this scene and deducing facts from that knowledge. It helped to shut off my emotions and view this as a puzzle, a game, and the players as objects. There'd be enough time for emotions later.

I broke it down into parts, examining them up close, but not touching. The trunk had been pried open—crowbar marks marred its edge. The girl wasn't bound—she'd either been drugged or forced in here by someone stronger than her. No bruises were visible on her wrists or ankles. Her dress was cheap, short, and covered in teal sequins. One of her black pumps was missing. She wore a heart-shaped necklace with "A" etched on it. There was a tattoo of a bird on her right ankle. The arrow was hand-fashioned from wood and feathers, but had no workman's logo. It had been driven into her heart by hand, judging from the angle. I swept my gaze over the scene one last time.

Then I took Timothy's hands and held them up to the light. That was the last piece of the puzzle.

"Call the police right now," I said in a tone that gave no room for disobedience.

He backed up. "What? I thought you were going to help me."

"I am helping you! We've got to get the county sheriff out here as soon as we can to document this."

He trembled.

"Timothy." I gave him a steady gaze. "You didn't do it—I can see that. Now let the law prove it." I pointed to his pocket, where his phone was. "Call and tell them you'd like to report a murder and a conspiracy."

He did as I said. After he had hung up, I turned to him. "Talk fast. Tell me what happened here."

"I woke up this morning, went to my car, and the door was unlocked. I always lock my car door. At first, I thought maybe some kids broke into take the radio or something."

"And you found her?"

"Yes, she was cold. I freaked and drove out here... I had to get away, to think of what to do."

"You called me and who else?"

He shook his head. "No one. I would never..." His voice cracked, and I saw the fear and sorrow in his eyes. "I want to hire you. I can pay whatever you want, but you have to help me. I know you think for yourself, that the truth is more important than the law sometimes. I need you to do whatever you can to find out what happened and keep me from losing everything."

I worried that this man knew me a little too well. His perception was good—maybe being a reporter gave him the ability to see through the article in the newspaper to the real story.

The sun beat down, warming my skin. Sweat trickled down my back and I wiped my forehead with my blouse sleeve. After staring at the girl for a few minutes, I had to look away. No matter who she was, she deserved more than this. Someone had treated her like an expendable pawn in their game to trap Timothy, and that made my blood run hot. This wasn't just about Timothy, or Dan, or my business—I had to find whoever did this. I had to teach them a lesson about what happens when they treat people like garbage.

Sirens wailed in the distance and my palms started sweating. "Is there anything else you can tell me that will help?"

The wind scattered up dust and I squinted through my lashes and pursed my lips. "Well?"

Timothy's eyes reddened and he cleared his throat. He undid a key from his key ring and handed it to me. "Get my laptop at my hotel room and read my notes on the women's shelter here. That was my story. I was about to blast some leaders for their lack of response to battered women." I leaned forward, not wanting to miss a word. "They want me out of the way. Also—" The police cars were getting closer. And I could see them off in the distance coming from both directions. "Talk to Yona."

A big white Ford truck with a magnetic red light on top pulled up, making dust and dirt fly. I shaded my eyes from the sun and watched as a leathery-faced officer got out. In big bold letters on the side if the truck, it read "Indian Tribal Police".

Two Idaho State troopers in black-and-white Chargers came from the opposite direction. They pulled to a stop. Four officers stepped out, but didn't make a move to come talk to us.

I grabbed Timothy's forearm. He looked at me intently. "Now you listen to me and do exactly what I tell you. Not a word—you don't tell them your name, not one breath. You got that?" He nodded. "Good. Now as far as they know, I'm your lawyer. Who knows if it will even matter, but we'll deal with it as it comes. Just remember, not a word. Make them need me. You only talk through me, understand?"

"Yes…" He hesitated. Then, as the officer approached us, he said quickly, "Just promise me something."

"Okay."

"Don't believe what they say about me."

CHAPTER 9

"COME WITH US, SIR." The older man wore a flat expression and didn't even glance my way. He pushed Timothy around and clicked handcuffs into place. He was of medium build, with long black hair pulled back in a ponytail. He took out a cell phone and dialed, tossing me a deadpan look. "Got two here and four pokers and one cold one. Set up room one and bring in Chaska. He's gonna want to be there for this."

The second Indian tribal police officer was a young boy of no more than twenty, I guessed. He stood by the truck, holding a shotgun, and appeared to be taking in the scene with more understanding than his age should have allowed. The anger on his face at the sight of the dead girl was palpable.

Joshua was talking with the state troopers. They looked bored and pissed all at the same time—they didn't have any authority on Indian land, but had to respond to the call anyway.

After a short back and forth, the ITP officer replaced the phone in his pocket and turned toward me. "And you are…?"

"Sarah Steele. I'm his lawyer. And that is my assistant." I motioned to Joshua, who was standing over by the state troopers.

"You realize you have no real say here, just what we give you." He spit and dug the tip of his boot in the dirt. "But I'm okay with it as long as you keep out of our way. Everyone deserves the chance to defend themselves."

I was taken aback. All my instincts were telling me I was in for a fight, and to hear him sounding like a caring human being made me wonder who this man was and if he could be an ally. "Thanks. I'll do all I can to abide by your laws."

"I can deal with that, Miss Steele. I'm Tahatan, head of security around here and head of the Indian Tribal Police. In terms you will understand, my only boss is the chief, Chaska Tate. You may find our ways strange, but no matter how you feel about it, when you're on Indian land, you're in our nation. What I say goes. My word is law around here. Got it?"

"Understood. May I ride with Timothy?" I asked. Tahatan looked at Timothy, who sat meekly at our feet just like I told him. I was glad he took my advice to heart.

"I see that I'm not going to get much out of him without you there. So, yeah, you can ride in the back with him."

"I'm going to go talk to the state police and my assistant. Can you give me a few minutes?"

"Just hurry it up. Them Pokers don't have a lick of business being here. They can watch all they like, but you tell them to go back to their caves and keep out of our affairs."

His dislike for them was thick. I wondered what had gone on to warrant such a feeling. I was sure I'd find out soon enough.

As I talked to Joshua and filled him in, I saw another pickup truck pull up. Two guys got out and began to take pictures of the body and the SUV.

Josh lowered his voice and took a few steps away from the state troopers. "So as far as I can tell, the police hate the Indians and the Indians hate the police. They have orders to note what happens, but only as observers," Josh said. The two were getting back into their cars and were about to head out.

"I told them we would keep them up-to-date and they seemed relieved. I don't think they like playing babysitter."

The state trooper eyed me and I gave Timothy a wave. He didn't respond. "I'm going to ride with Timothy. Can you follow us and call Mandy?"

"Sure, but why do you want me to call her?"

"Because this is our company's first case, and if you're in, so's Mandy."

Josh nodded. "Does she know that?"

"She will after you tell her," I said.

CHAPTER 10

WHEN OFFICER TAHATAN SAID I could ride in the back, I
assumed he meant the back seat of his quad cab truck. I was wrong.
Lowering the tailgate, he motioned for us to get in. Then he took out
a second pair of handcuffs and looped one to an eyehook in the bed
and the other to Timothy's ankle.

I put my hands on my hips. "You can't be serious."

Tahatan raised one eyebrow and slammed the tailgate shut. I sat
down next to Timothy and groaned. "Well, this day is not going like
I thought it would. Most guys would at least buy me dinner before
inviting me to go to jail with them."

"I know a good place, but you're going to have to take a rain
check. I'm a little tied up right now." He laughed at his lame joke, and I
was glad he was keeping his spirits up.

"At least you have a sense of humor." I checked my phone and
saw a text from Solomon. He was going to be home tonight and wanted
to come over. My skin warmed at the thought of seeing him. I got a
twinge of regret when I texted him that I'd be out tonight, but I'd catch
up with him tomorrow—regret that I wasn't a normal person who

could welcome her boyfriend home with a normal night of Chinese and making out on the couch. With a sigh, I texted See you tomorrow and put away my phone.

Solomon did something to me that I couldn't deny. We had chemistry, and the more I got to know him, the more I liked him. But I was on a case, and determined to see things through even if it meant not welcoming Solomon back with open arms. That was the price, and it was worth it. A girl was dead, and that trumped my boyfriend.

I pierced Timothy with a stare. "Time to tell me a story. We're alone, and I am not sure we'll have this luxury again anytime soon." The truck started and we pulled out onto the highway.

Timothy started talking loud enough for me to hear over the road noise, but not loud enough for them to hear inside the truck. "I've been researching sexual abuse in Indian communities for a story. There is a high rate of rape and domestic abuse. Almost all of it goes unpunished. Out of the fifty-three cases of rape and sexual abuse reported last year, only one man was convicted and thrown in jail."

The truck hit a pothole and I bounced, hitting my backside hard. "Ow." The wind made it hard to talk, but Timothy leaned close to my ear so I could hear him.

"Nice transportation, huh?"

I grimaced.

"Anyway, I did most of my research online, but I had to finish it up on the ground. I flew in ten days ago from my hometown in Chicago. I've been staying at the casino hotel, and that's where it got interesting. At first, I thought this was just going to be about women being abused and the men getting away with it. But once I got here, I discovered it went much deeper than that."

"What do you mean?" I yelled above the wind.

"Sex trafficking, drugs, money laundering—the works. There have been three casinos built in three years. All of them are used to move girls and drugs in and out. All the tribe members work for the casinos, and the income supports the entire tribe. I was really getting some good info when suddenly, the witnesses shut down. Someone scared them— scared them bad because no one will talk to me."

I nodded. It was a common story, one I'd heard a hundred times. It was why corruption went on unhindered.

He cleared his throat. "I had one woman, a local writer, who was trying to help me, but now no one will even look at me, let alone talk to me. I was told to leave, the hotel doubled my room rate, and I got a note under my door yesterday telling me that I was in danger, that if I stayed and kept asking questions, someone would die."

The thought hit me and I kicked myself for not asking sooner. "Did you know the girl?"

"Yeah, she was one of the good ones. Her name is Lina Sever. She was being abused by her father and talked to me three days ago. She died because of me."

CHAPTER 11

THE TOWN OF LITTLE Bear was a joke. It was as if someone built three huge casinos out in the middle of the desert and then had a road put in. Despite the remote location and the odd setup, the large parking lots were all full. Business was good.

The rest of the town was located past the neon lights and glittering signs. Small row houses lined the main street. There was one way in and one way out, making this a dead end.

We turned down a dirt lane that wrapped around and opened up to the back of the largest casino, the Golden Nugget. Parking next to a black BMW 5 series, I waited for our great and mighty god to come and give us permission to get out.

"Remember, don't say anything unless I tell you to."

Timothy nodded. He was pale and his hands trembled. That was good. I wanted him to stay afraid, as this was no light matter. Of course, I didn't want him bawling on my shoulder, either. So I said reassuringly, "We're going to work this out. Just you wait."

Both truck doors opened and the young boy opened the tailgate. Tahatan removed the handcuffs from the eyehook and Timothy's ankle.

"All right, both of you get on out of there."

It had only been a twenty-minute ride from the old café to here, but my body ached as if I had just played tackle football with a bunch of jacked-up Texans.

"Don't you have an ITP building or a jail?" I asked.

Tahatan spit nasty chew out the side of his mouth and grinned, showing flecks of the stuff in his teeth. "Don't need one. We have it all right here in the Golden Nugget. You see, it's not just a casino and hotel. In the main lobby is everything you need—day spa, mini mall, food court, and we even have a post office."

"So you'll be keeping Timothy in the spa, then?" Sarcasm probably wasn't my best move at the moment, but I couldn't help it.

He grunted, and his mouth twitched. Was that a smile?

I kept going. "What about other city essentials—a gas station, food market, courthouse, dungeon, and such? Every good casino has a dungeon, right?"

He spit again and looked at me out of the corner of his eye. "All here. The lower floors are where the real action is. Courthouse, our offices, and even the jail—you may call it the dungeon if you wish. As far as the other stuff goes, across the street at the Silver Mine, they have a local food market, and the Bronze Star has a full-service gas station."

I whistled. "Wow, you have quite the setup here. It's like the casinos are the town."

The back door opened, and a skinny man in a guard uniform stiffened and avoided eye contact with Tahatan. Speeding past us, he left in a hurry, keeping his head down. Tahatan had these people running scared—maybe he was God.

"The original town of Little Bear had two main streets with a small market, one gas pump, and a few other outbuildings, but all that's left of it is what you saw on the way in—some cheap houses and a few old school members who won't adapt with the times. The rest of the tribe is scattered about on plots of land from here to about one hundred miles thataway." He pointed south.

Ushering us past another guard, he took the lead and we walked down a wide hallway to a bank of elevators. Someone with style had designed the casino. The lighting was low, the art was modern, and the accents were bold but not too much. I bet this drew every bored housewife with a good nose for brandy and money for blackjack from the surrounding four states. Appetizing smells wafted through the lobby, making my mouth water. Were those chocolate chip cookies on the counter? I grabbed one and started munching. Mmm, it tasted fresh from the oven, and the chocolate was still gooey. Although I'd never been one who enjoyed casinos, the atmosphere made me relax. Pass me a martini and I just might hand over all my money. I gulped. I'd better stiffen up or my client might rot in jail while I got really good at craps.

We went down two floors and into one of the nicest offices I'd ever seen.

"This is the courthouse, jail, and headquarters for the Indian Tribal Police." He tipped his hat to a couple of men who were talking and sipping coffee. They stared back at Timothy, their eyes glinting in anger. So they'd already heard why we were here. I studied each one—memorized their faces and took in as much as I could from their mannerisms and their desks. One of these guys might have framed Timothy. From here on out, I couldn't trust anyone. Not even Timothy. Especially not Timothy. He had the most on the line.

We followed Tahatan back to a room with one door and a big one-way mirror. Inside were a single table and two chairs. Tahatan motioned. "Have a seat. Get comfortable. I'll have my man show your big friend into the waiting area."

I couldn't let him get the last word. Widening my eyes, I said with a pert smile, "I'd be a lot more comfortable if you brought me a latte."

He snorted and slammed the door shut. Looked like my petition was lost on him.

I sat down on one of the cold metal chairs and Timothy started pacing the room. His hands were still cuffed behind his back. I had to pee, but I was afraid they'd start grilling Timothy if I left him for one moment.

And there was still so much I didn't know. It set me on edge—I was the person who liked to have three truckloads of information and research on a case before I even took it. This was out of my comfort zone. "Okay, what's going on with this place? It's nicer than some of the places in Vegas. Color me impressed."

"How many holding rooms in Vegas have you been to?" he asked.

I gave him a deadpan look.

Timothy chuckled. "I know. These casinos are stylish and brand spanking new. This is the main one, but all three are nice. They went all out and that's half the reason people drive clear out here to gamble. They have some of the highest payouts of any Casino in the U.S."

"And all the money goes back to the tribe?" That couldn't be all bad. More money for education, social services, roads, and other ways to improve the tribe's quality of life. At least, that was it in theory. Did they really put the money where it should be?

Timothy's shoulders tightened. "Its a scam, that's what it is, and the reason why I'm even in this room. None of the money reaches the town, and people suffer because of it."

"Wait, hold up. You're telling me that once the State recognized their tribal status, they got free land and money just for being Indian? When?"

"It wasn't until the 60s, when Chief Hara Tate proved this was their original land and fought to get it back. He was a hero. And when he died, his son, Chaska, continued his work. This land was stolen from them in the first place, not to mention that most of their civilization was almost wiped out several times. We owe them more than land and

money, but that's another story for another day." He sighed. "Once
they had the land and official status, they set up their laws. So it was
all going well until Chaska and his best friend, Takota Watters, had a
falling out—over a girl, nonetheless."

"How romantic," I said dryly.

"The fight was on. It was family against family, each trying to
take control of the council, who can do just about anything they want
without consulting the tribe. And the chief has final say on the council."

"Who's in control now?"

Timothy sat on the chair next to mine. "Chaska Tate. He owns the
town and has had the council for years, but this is an election year. His
former best friend is running this next term, though. He's the reason the
casinos are making money. In a few weeks, they hold the elections, so
things are supercharged."

I scratched my fingernail against the table. "How does the best
friend make all the money?"

"See, Chaska is loved by the people. He keeps everyone happy
and things have been peaceful, for the most part, under his eye. But
Takota Watters is one smart businessman. He went off to an Ivy League
college and came back and started the Golden Nugget casino—which,
at the time, was a dive bar with a few slots. Everyone employed at the
casino, which is basically everyone in town, reports to him."

So Chaska owned the government and Watters owned the trade.
"So what's the problem? If they work together—Chaska takes care
of social and legislative matters and the Watters guy makes them all
money—everybody wins." Even as I said it, I knew what power did—it
made people hungry for more.

"You'd think, but they hate each other. And with Takota Watters
controlling the casinos and Chaska controlling the council, they're at
war. If Watters takes the council, Chaska won't stand for it and the
whole tribe will be split, broken, and maybe never recover."

I rubbed my temples. "I think I'm following you, but how would he get rid of Chaska? They have tribal rights."

"Yeah, every approved member gets a share of the profits. And most of them work for the casino in some way, so they're getting paid a wage on top of their royalty. Wait till you see the houses they live in. All around here in the foothills, you'll find million-dollar homes, pools, and parks, and all the Watters are on one side of the river and all Chaska Tate's people are on the other."

"I gotta find me a nice Indian boy to marry." I touched my ring finger.

"Good luck. You ready for the end game?"

"Of course. This is getting interesting."

"For the past few months, Watters has been calling into question the blood rights of the members. The council is making members prove their bloodline."

Then it hit me—the play, the final blow that would destroy one family and leave the other that much richer. "They're kicking members out—fewer people at the table means bigger pieces of pie. And they've been using any means necessary." I eyed him. From his history of peacekeeping and social justice, I could see how this story appealed to him—but everyone had secrets, and Timothy hadn't told me any yet. There had to be more to this story. "Now, how the heck did you get tangled up in this?"

He stared at the black window. "Penchant for trouble, I guess."

"I'm not buying that. Give me more." I leaned forward, trying to see his eyes. They were sad, almost haunted. My heart turned for him. "There's a dead girl in your trunk. How did it get to that?"

"She was one of my leads." His voice broke. "And now she's dead."

Heavy footsteps came from the hallway. We both looked up. They were coming.

CHAPTER 12

A MAN BURST THROUGH the door. He was a red-faced man in a cream-colored cowboy hat and thick bottle-cap glasses. His hair was black with white streaks, thick and shiny, and his face was worn and weathered, as if he had been through his share of storms.

Tahatan followed him in, but his mannerisms had changed. He was not the highest authority in the room anymore. His expression was meek and wary.

The tall man pointed at me and said to Tahatan, "I don't care who she is. Get her out of here and throw him in a cell."

"He deserves a defense. You of all people should know that."

The big man in a cowboy hat—I gathered this was the chief—came unglued. "You dare say that to me? After I've been the one defending you to everyone? I say who is guilty, I say who deserves what. You got that? Now do as I say or so help me, your name will be the next one called."

Tahatan swallowed hard and shot a look at me that I couldn't read. It was time to speak up.

"I am going to assume that you're the man in charge—Chief

Chaska Tate."

He spun toward me and opened his mouth to respond, but I cut in before he could.

"Look here, Chief. I get that you say jump and the world says 'how high'. But I have some information for you. This man, Timothy James, is innocent. You'll easily be able to deduce it from the evidence—it didn't take me more than five minutes of looking at the scene and I'm sure your men are twice as sharp as I am, right? He didn't kill that girl, and we both know it." I stood up and squared my shoulders. "Now we can do this the easy way or the hard way."

He narrowed his eyes, but I didn't look away. I wouldn't let him intimidate me. "You a lawyer?"

"Yes, sir." I braced myself for the barrage of abuse most people heaped on lawyers. But he surprised me.

"Then you should know that the easy way is not always the best way. I don't get to think just about Timothy's innocence or guilt. I have an entire society to consider."

Timothy froze, and his eyes revealed the panic he felt. My mind cleared, and the same feeling I had fighting the gang of men in Rio washed over me. It was as if this darkness in me liked to be in a fighting position. I should be scared, terrified because I was outnumbered and confronting men who had more authority and power than I'd ever have.

But sometimes what is flies in the face of what should be.

Taking a step toward Chaska, I lowered my voice to a growl. "Now, I know I have no authority here, but if you do not give that beautiful, dead young lady some justice, your quiet little operation here might not be so quiet anymore. The last thing you want is outsiders snooping around, checking up on you, interviewing people, writing articles, gathering an audience. Timothy and I are not just two people. We have access to thousands of listening ears. So I suggest you let me do what I do best and give my client a fair shake."

The room fell silent. Chaska puffed out his chest and seemed to calm a touch. "Well, maybe I did come on a little strong. There's no need to be fighting when all anyone is interested in is the truth."

I leaned back, flickering a smile. "I'm glad we see it the same way."

Chaska took off his hat and wiped the sweat from his forehead. "Now, miss, what is your name?"

"Steele. Sarah Steele."

CHAPTER 13

AFTER THREE HOURS OF back and forth with Tahatan and Chaska Tate, we were no closer to any sort of agreement. By their law, they could hold Timothy for up to three years on a charge, so things were not looking good. They put him in a holding cell, and I had Tahatan promise he'd call me if anything new happened or if they needed to speak to Timothy again. I wanted to believe that he'd keep his word.

I had Joshua call Dan to let him know that he was right and we couldn't get our office involved due to tribal law, but that I would keep him updated on the case. I speed walked out of that place, my mind buzzing. There was so much to do. I had at least six mental lists running through my head. Joshua had the car waiting for me in the circular drive. I pulled my notebook from my purse and started scribbling my notes feverishly.

Joshua pulled onto the highway. "Watch it. Your pen might start smoking any moment."

Biting my lip, I finished. "There. We have so many leads and so much research to do, I'm afraid I'm going to have to hire this out to foreign markets. Do you know any good research teams in India?"

"Very funny. Now where do you want to go?"

"I don't think we can do anything more here tonight," I said.

He pulled into a gas station in front of the Silver Mine. We got out and I stretched, walking along the curb. Little white flowers poked out of the sandy dirt—specks of beauty in the drab ground. I picked one and twirled it between my fingers, thinking. The wind blew my hair across my shoulders and I shivered. It was getting chilly.

I needed coffee. The beverage they had in the gas station pot resembled engine oil that had been scraped off the pavement outside, so I opted for some canned caffeine. I also grabbed Joshua's favorite candy bar, and a bag of pistachios for me.

Joshua was just putting the gas pump back in its cradle when I walked up. "I want to get Mandy up-to-speed on our little plan and see what she thinks. Is there any way you can write my resignation for me, and on the drive back I'll tell you the story?" I handed him his snack and drink.

He snorted and then laughed. "Are you serious?"

"Dead serious. I want to be on the phone all night—I know some Indian rights lawyers and tribe advocates and I need to get their perspectives. Writing a resignation for Dan Wandering Eyes is the last thing I can do tonight. I wouldn't know how to tie my shoes if it weren't for you. You're my sun, my moon, my starlit sky—"

He held up his hand. "Okay, okay. I'm on it. Should I add in your trademark snark and a few memes just for the fun of it?"

I unshelled a couple of pistachios and popped them in my mouth. "Of course. And don't forget to misspell several words. That's another of my trademarks."

Josh ate his candy bar in two bites. "Sure. That's what I am here for, boss—to do your bidding." He laughed. The sound was deep and comforting.

"Good. I'm glad we're on the same page."

After filling up at the gas station, I took in the sights. It was an odd thing to see three huge hotels and casinos sitting out here in the middle of the desert. They lit up the sky, and neon lights of every color accosted the natural surroundings. All of them were beautiful, and I noticed for the first time a new golf course being put in up on a small bluff. They were going all out.

"Not quite right, is it?" Josh said as he began the process of squeezing his large body into my car.

"No, it's not. It's like a movie set or something. Like it'll all blow away in a few weeks' time."

After we were on the road, I started going over this mess I found myself in.

"So what's the plan, boss?"

I punched him in the arm and he pretended to be hurt. "Enough with the boss crap. I am your boss, but you say it all stupid, like you're mocking me."

"'Cause I am."

"I thought so. I talked to Mr. James, and he has agreed to my terms. Dan will cover the rather hefty price quote I put on the case. I told him that we would act like personal assistants, but cover all fronts."

"So what are we going to call this band of misfits?"

"Hey, speak for yourself. We're the people you call when you're in need of the best. Between the three of us, we can do just about anything. You're one of the best researchers I've ever seen, and Mandy can hack into anything."

"And you're a shark when it comes to finding the truth and getting people to do what you want."

"I'm glad you can see my skills clearly, young one."

Staring out the window, I let my mind wander. Sometimes the

best way to think is not to settle on one idea and to see where the paths lead. The landscape went hazy—trees and grasses and shrubs blurred together until it was so dark that I could only see the stars glistening above the tree line.

By the end of the road, I'd decided on my own path in all this. And like most things in my life, it was going to be messy.

CHAPTER 14

MY SUITCASE SAT ON my bed, mocking me. The last thing
I wanted to do was unpack, but I had lugged it onto my bed so I
couldn't procrastinate and now I started sorting clothes into piles.
That mundane task set my mind free to think about the case.

"Now, girlie, how're you going to solve this murder? And try to do
it without killing someone this time, aye?"

I knew that talking to myself was not the sanest thing in the world,
but I lived alone and I needed someone to talk to—even if it was me.
Though, sometimes I wasn't the best conversationalist.

Facts. That was what I was craving—like an adrenaline junkie
craved their next fix, except nerdier. Dialing my friend, Simone Nelson
at the Bureau of Indian Affairs, I got her on the first ring. She had been
my workout partner in law school.

"Sarah! It's been a long time. Bet you've gone soft," she said.
"Need me to fly over and remind you what a real workout is?"

"Oh, please," I said. "The only thing you taught me was where the
five-pound weights were. I didn't know gyms even had them."

We bantered back and forth a bit until I told her about the case. She gave a long sigh after I ended, which gave me a bad feeling.

"You're not gonna like what I have to say."

I braced myself. "Hit me."

"The Justice Department is in charge of prosecuting most of the more serious crimes on the reservations, but they only file charges in about half of all murder charges, and take only one-third of all rape cases."

"What?" I gasped. "That's preposterous."

"I know. So even if the ITP filed this murder charge, there's only a fifty-percent chance that the Justice Department would take it to court."

My throat tightened. Here was another place where Lady Justice was not only blindfolded, but she was bound and gagged too. That meant that the murdered girl wasn't going to be the only one with no justice—Timothy wouldn't get any either.

"What can I do for my client? They still think he killed her, and he's been jailed."

She paused and then said, "That's not right. Only a federally certified agent has that right. Was there an FBI man there?"

"No!" My voice rose in glee. "There wasn't. We have them—they illegally detained a non-Indian. Heck, I could even charge them with kidnapping."

"But be careful," she said. "Everything's a lot more complicated on the rez."

"You know me. Careful is my middle name."

She scoffed.

"Thank you so much!" I threw some shirts in the washer while I spoke. "Anything I can do for you, let me know."

"Fly over and visit me and I'll whip your butt in spinning class. That'll be thanks enough."

I smiled and hung up, mulling over what she'd said. Then I spent the next hour unpacking and tossing clothes into the washing machine.

The same thoughts kept buzzing through my head, so I turned up the radio and danced around the room pretending I was on The Voice. Things around me weren't perfect, but I suddenly felt good about my life, as if the storm was where I belonged. That was the magic of music.

Spinning around, I flipped my hair back and belted out the chorus to the One Republic song that was playing. I screeched in surprise when I saw Solomon leaning against the doorjamb to my bedroom.

"Now that's hot," he said with a lopsided grin.

My hand was over my heart and I gasped, and then laughed. "Goodness, boy, you scared me. What are you doing here? I mean, how did you get in? And what a jerk! Couldn't you call or text or something? Or knock? God, the least you could do was knock." I was rambling, and he didn't move. He just looked at me as if I was the most amusing thing he'd ever seen. I couldn't stop. "How long have you been standing there? I can't believe you ..." I was embarrassed and flushed all at the same time. Solomon grabbed my hand, pulling me into his arms.

He kissed me, and my head cleared of all my questions. There were times when I wanted to fight him, to pull away because of my own fear, but in his arms all I could do was give my heart to him over and over again.

"I missed you," he said.

"I missed you too." I kissed him again, and he held me close. Our bodies fit together like two long-lost puzzle pieces. I loved the way he smelled, the warmth of his body, how he was the perfect mix of hard and soft, strong and gentle.

Pressing my hands on his chest, I leaned away from him. "When did ... How did you get in?" My mind was not helping me out. Thanks a lot, Benedict Arnold.

"You left your door... unlocked?" He gave a cheesy grin. "And if it was locked, well, I'm the FBI, and I've been trained in the art of lock picking." He looked like a little boy when he was teasing me. I melted.

"Maybe I should get a dog. With big teeth."

"Dogs love me."

He slid his hand behind my head and kissed me hard. A tingle shot up my body, starting at my feet and ending at the top of my head, leaving goose bumps all over my skin.

We settled into the couch and I let him take the stress of the day from me. I wanted him, to be with him, but my mind was my best friend and worst enemy. Tonight I wondered which role it would take on.

CHAPTER 15

MY CHEST WAS TIGHT. Each breath was work, and it hurt all the way through into my spine. I was stressed, and the pressure made me want to run. To run away and never look back.

Mom was in the kitchen cooking dinner. She saw me sitting at the table and gave me the look that said so much more than words ever could.

Do it. Do it or you'll be next. If I do, it's all on you.

I knew it was a dream—or was it a memory? It was hard to tell. I was a little kid—I can't remember how old. Five or seven?

Mom sliced celery so fast that I lost myself watching her hands move with precision. She turned and glanced at me again with the same look. Her eyes were hard, but deep down they were sad. A dark purple bruise surrounded her left eye and a new one was beginning to show on her cheek. I jumped when a rough voice came from the living room.

"Sarah, what's taking you so long? It's just Scotch. Pour it in a glass, one ice cube. You know how I want it. Now quit dawdling and hurry up. Sarah Ann!" His voice was harsh and grew more insistent.

"Sarah, answer me."

"Coming, Dad."

He muttered something, but all I could make out was "Lazy kid …
stupid …"

I stared at the glass sitting in front of me on the table. It was half
full, one cube of ice. Next to it was a small glass bottle with a dropper. I
knew what it was, knew what Mom wanted.

Tears ran down my cheeks and I couldn't breathe. I knew I had to
move, to pick up the glass and bring it into the living room where my
dad sat in his old recliner. The TV would be on, and he would have an
old tobacco pipe in his hand and bruises on his knuckles.

Dad hollered, and I heard the recliner pop as he released the
footrest.

I moved. Grabbing the glass, I ran into the dark, smoke-filled
living room. His face was red. He snatched the glass from my hand and
tossed back the drink. His dark hair was matted and he glared at me. He
opened his mouth to say something, but closed it and his face softened.
"Come here, Bits. Give me a hug."

I burst into tears.

A rush of emotion snapped me awake and I realized I was crying.
Solomon was stroking my hair, holding me and gently whispering, "It's
okay. It was a bad dream. I'm here. It's okay…"

My body shook uncontrollably, and sweat soaked through my
T-shirt and panties. It was dark in my room and so I let the tears rage.
I wanted to lock that part of my heart away forever and hide from
everything and everyone.

Slowly I got control back and remembered that I'd fallen asleep in
Solomon's arms. He had never stayed over before and I really wanted
to want him too, but something stopped me—my dang overthinking
mind stopped me. I must have been a lot more tired than I thought
because the last thing I remembered was him holding me and telling

me about his trip home. I felt so safe in his arms, as if nothing else mattered. Then I woke in my nightmare, the one I would never be able to escape.

CHAPTER 16

HOTAH WATCHED THE WHORE get dressed and played with the scar above his right eyebrow. It was a mark, one he would never let himself forget. It was his first attempt to kill himself during the worst winter of his life. Even the light had seemed dark then, and he'd lost his way. After he'd returned from a hunt empty handed, he'd shot one arrow straight up into the air and waited for it to drive itself home. It hit him, but it didn't fracture his skull. Turned out he was only good at killing other people.

She dressed as if she had somewhere to be. Hotah imagined that he was good with the ladies, and he was often confused as to why some resisted him like this.

"You like how I make you feel, baby?"

The tiny blonde turned, pulled up her mini skirt, and half smiled, flipping her hair. "Yeah, you were the best I've ever had." She picked up her high heels and gave a small giggle. At first, Hotah thought she was serious and her giggle was due to his charm, but then it dawned on him that she could be mocking him.

Maybe she needed to be taught some respect. "Watch it, slut. I'm an important man around here—you know who I am?" Hotah slid his hand under the covers, reaching for his knife.

"Of course, Hotah. Everyone knows who you are. Your face is on every sign from here to Boise," she said from the bathroom, her tone still mocking as if she thought he was some dumb pre-pubescent boy.

"You're the world-famous trick shooter in the Wild Wild West play at the Golden Nugget. No one's better."

He gripped the knife tighter. "It's not a play, it's a show, one of the best shows around—even better than Vegas! Everyone says that. And I'm the star, I'm famous, and you act like I'm just some John."

She shuffled from the bathroom and scooped up her shirt, purse, and coat. "What do you want from me? I made you happy, you had a good time—what more do you want?"

Hotah threw the knife at her. She screamed, covering her mouth with both hands as she dropped her purse. The knife buried itself into the wall next to her head and plaster dusted her shoulder. She bent down and grabbed her purse, shaking like a scared rabbit.

"I meant to miss," he reassured her, hoping she wouldn't tell her handler. He liked the lineup of girls and didn't want to jack up his personal play time.

She slammed the door, and Hotah cursed. Aw, who cared—no one would believe a second-rate whore. Who did she think she was? He was somebody, a star, a killer, and soon, a member of the council. She was just paid entertainment.

Getting dressed in a dirty T-shirt and jeans, he took the elevator to the Watering Hole. It was one of the casino bars, and his favorite. He drank for free, a perk of being a valuable member of the tribe.

"Jack and Coke, Buck."

Buck was the shirtless bartender. It wasn't his real name, but the customers liked it.

"You believe these girls?" Hotah motioned to three giggle-factory girls at the end of the bar. They were flirting with some soft city guy. "You'd think they'd know a good thing when it was right there in front of them. Guess they just want the dregs."

Buck put a drink in front of him and grunted. "You working tonight?"

Hotah tossed back his drink and wiped his mouth. "Do I look like I'm working tonight? Do you see me wearing a feather in my hair? Do you see my bow and arrow?"

Buck held up his hands in surrender. "Sorry. Just askin', brother."

"I'm not your bro." Hotah threw his glass at Buck and missed. It shattered against the wall. Buck wiped his mouth with the back of his hand and his whole upper body flexed.

A moment later, two big men in suits came up behind Hotah. He saw them coming in the big mirror behind the bar and he rubbed his scar, hoping they would lay a hand on him.

"Time to go, hotshot. Party's over." They grabbed him and pulled him from his barstool.

"Get off me. Do you know who I am? I'll have your jobs … Come on, Buck." He realized he could lose his favorite drinking spot if Buck had any lasting hard feelings. "Hey, I didn't mean nothing." He twisted, and the two men released his arms. He smoothed his T-shirt and looked each man up and down. He could take them. Maybe he should—teach them that it was never okay to cross a man like him.

"Wise choice." He nodded at them. "Now go guard something." He took a swing at the shorter of the two and connected, but the big man didn't seem to care. He even winked one eye as if he was happy to get a fist to the face.

"That's it? That's your best punch?" He rubbed his jaw and looked to the other bouncer. They grinned, grabbed Hotah, and dragged him from the bar.

"Let me go," Hotah screamed, and the packed bar watched him. It was the looks on their faces—they were all smirking, mocking.

"You have no idea who I am, what I can do. I killed a girl—shot her in the chest. You think you can just throw me out?"

"Easy, tiger."

"Keep talking, twinkle toes."

Hotah stumbled out into the parking lot and the two bouncers laughed. "Now sober up before your next show and consider this bar off limits from now on."

Hotah spit and reached for his knife. But it was not in his hip holster like it was supposed to be—he must have left it upstairs. He stared at the bouncer he punched and made a mental note to come back later to kill him. No one made Hotah look like a fool, especially not a ten-dollar-an-hour bouncer.

CHAPTER 17

BREAKFAST WAS JUST WHAT I needed to forget about my awful nightmare. Solomon and I met Mandy at Berryhill Bacon downtown. While waiting for Joshua, Mandy and I ordered, and Solomon got a black coffee to go.

It felt great not to wear formal business wear like I had to at the office. Since the men at ITP weren't wearing suits, I wasn't going to dress up, furthering my outsider look. Instead, I opted for tailored black pants, comfortable flats, and a simple blouse. Usually I wore heels so I could be taller—it lent to more people taking me seriously. But this time, I was confident I could get what I wanted without them.

What I wanted was Solomon's advice on the case, but he had to jet off to his FBI job and I was starving. I gave the short version on the car ride over and asked him who the FBI contact was at the rez. This would all be figured out soon.

Solomon sent a few texts and found out who was assigned to the tribe. It was someone named Watters. My heart sank. No wonder the FBI had no clue what was going on—they had an agent who was in the family.

"There has to be another agent, right?" I asked. "How could one man be assigned to the whole town?"

"Well…" Solomon shrugged. "Money is always tight. And if they have one agent who's handling things, why send another?"

"Yeah, handling things." I gritted my teeth.

Our food came in record time, and Mandy began her divide-and-destroy method of eating. "Geez, this is amazing. Have you have you tried this sage-and-honey bacon? It's like a party in my mouth." Her cheeks pooched out as she chomped away, and I tried to look as disgusted as I felt.

"You're eating like it's the end of the world. Try chewing first." I handed her a napkin. "And you've got some syrup on your chin."

"I am chewing," Mandy said with her mouth full. She had her hair up in a messy bun today with a drumstick rammed through it like a spear. Honest to God, a drumstick. She must have taken it from Rick's drum set.

Taking a sip of my coconut latte, I opened the file Joshua had brought. He was up at the counter ordering his food, and even though he was late, he acted all hurt because we didn't wait to order. The file had some background information on the dead girl, Lina Sever. Age 21. I was surprised at how emotional I was over this. She was so young— too young. Joshua was good at his job. He had copies of her driver's license, public record, history of residence, and a list of next of kin. I slid the file to Mandy, and she pawed though it with her sticky fingers.

"You can keep that copy," I said, a little annoyed. "So you know how we've talked about doing our own thing?"

Mandy nodded. "Yeah—like Nancy Drew, but cooler. Joshua told me all about your mess of a case. Way to start us off right, Sarah."

"Yeah, well, try not to let it bother you too much. This is how it goes. If it was easy, anyone could do it. I talked to Joshua, and I think that between the three of us, we can cover all the bases. Maybe pick up one more person for grunt work down the line—"

She put the file down and gaped at me. "Whoa, hold up. You mean you're quitting your job? I thought this was extra—you know, a spare time kind of thing?"

Though I didn't know why, I was suddenly embarrassed about my job situation. "More or less."

But Mandy saw right through me. "Sarah, what happened?"

I glanced at Solomon, who was standing over by the window reading something on his phone. "I've been asked to resign. My history is too dirty for their clean halls."

"What?" Mandy screeched, then looked around and lowered her voice. "That douche bag fired you?"

At the memory of Dan's face, I was suddenly glad I didn't have to go clock in that day. "He still wants to work with me, of course. He's footing this bill. But he wants to keep me on at a distance. You know how he is when it comes to bad press. I thought we could take the opportunity and run with it."

Mandy's eyes sharpened and she leaned back in her chair.

I continued. "We'll see where it goes." I finished the last of my latte and ordered another. "You never know—might be the start of something fun."

Mandy gave me the "I see through all your B.S." look and sighed. "So what are we gonna call this agency or whatever? We need a rockin' name, like the Three Avengers or the ND Crime Fighting Crew."

Solomon walked over, bent down, and kissed me. "I gotta go. Let me know later what your evening looks like." He nodded to Mandy, and she smiled like an idiot.

When he was gone, she blinked at me and sipped her orange juice. "What a hunk."

I made a face and laughed. "Yes, he is. And as for your other thing … Uh, no. We're not a girl band, and if we want to get high-level cases, we have to come across as professionals."

Joshua sat down. "We are professionals, but what are we offering? I don't even have a clear idea of what we are doing, so how can we sell it to the public?"

"We offer awesomeness," Mandy exclaimed.

I ignored her. "We can't offer legal counsel in other states and I don't want to be just another law firm. We're the people who get things done behind the scenes, the fixers. You have a problem, who you gonna call...?"

We all three looked at each other, and it was Joshua who broke down first. "Ghostbusters," he whispered.

CHAPTER 18

I'D MEMORIZED EVERYTHING IN Lina's file, but I went over it one more time in case I missed something. The picture on her driver's license showed a smiling, fresh-faced girl. Joshua sat in the passenger seat of my car and kept looking over at me like I was a pot ready to boil.

"No, Josh, I'm not going to talk about it." I knew that in some ways, my job gave me my identity, and with it slipping through my fingers, I didn't know how I felt about myself.

"I didn't ask."

"Your silent asking is just as annoying. I'll be fine." I bit my fingernail absentmindedly.

"Your last two weeks have been crazy, enough to make anyone have to see psychologists for the rest of their life."

"I'm fine. And I've had psychologists in my face my whole life. I've memorized exactly what they'd say in this situation." I snapped the file shut. "I'm fine."

"You are far from fine, but if you don't want to talk about it, that's fine too." He shook his head, and his big cheeks jiggled like Jell-O.

"Fine."

We were twenty minutes out from the reservation, and I had Mandy doing research from her place. I didn't want her in the line of fire in case things went south.

"So we're really doing this consulting gig?" Joshua asked.

"Ready or not, here we come."

Joshua said nothing. After a minute of silence, he nodded. "Okay,"

"Okay."

I smiled and looked out the window. Sometimes life seemed nothing more than a shower of unfortunate events, but with Joshua, Mandy, and Solomon, I felt like I'd be okay.

CHAPTER 19

TAHATAN CHEWED ON A toothpick and had his feet up on his cluttered desk. I'd gone straight to see him when we got to the reservation. Country music was playing on the radio, and a basketball game was on the big screen TV mounted on the wall.

"You can't just hold Timothy. You've got to charge him with something," I said, restraining my voice.

He smiled and went back to reading the newspaper. "Those aren't the rules here, Miss Steele," he said offhandedly.

"According to your own laws—I looked it up—in the case of a murder, rape, or abuse of a minor, you have to inform the FBI."

Tahatan didn't even act surprised. He kept on reading. Why was he suddenly so aloof? "The FBI has been informed, and Special Agent Watters is looking into the situation." His voice was flat, unimpressed.

"I would like to talk to him."

"No."

"I need to see Timothy James."

"No."

"You can't deny me access to my client. He hired me to act on his behalf."

Tahatan lowered his paper and looked at Joshua and me. He seemed to consider what I was saying and then shook his head. "No."

I shifted my weight, about to lose my temper, when someone spoke from the doorway. "Now, now, let's not get into a fighting match again." Chaska stood behind us, holding his cowboy hat and chewing on something. "I don't see the harm in letting her talk to her... What is he, your client? Or are you two a thing?" He grinned, showing stained teeth and flecks of chew ground in between.

He was poking at me, trying to push my buttons. Well, he'd have to do a lot more than that. "I would like to talk to him. And if we're going to find out what really happened to Lina Sever I need to be free to investigate."

Tahatan stood up. "Not going to happen. We have it under control."

Chaska held up a hand, and Tahatan clamped his mouth shut. "The FBI is in charge here. If he's good with Miss Steele helping out, who are we to get in the way of justice? Besides, he is guilty. Mr. James was seen snooping around, bothering our people, and even made a few threats. He had her body in the back of his SUV, and he was the last one to talk to her. Maybe they fought, things got out of hand—who knows—but this is a simple case, so there's no need to make it more complicated than it has to be."

So he was playing both sides. I knew deep down there was a heart in there, that a part of him really cared about his tribe and who really killed Lina Sever. Or did he want to keep Timothy quiet and deal with the murderer on his own?

"Yona, will you please show Miss Steele to Mr. James's cell?" Chaska Tate said over his shoulder. A thin woman with jet-black hair and a gorgeous green silk wrap-around dress came into view. She smiled politely.

"This way," she said in almost a whisper.

Walking past Chaska, I motioned for Joshua, who was waiting out in the lobby. He hefted himself out of the chair he was crushing and followed me and Yona down a long hallway. She looked back at us and seemed to be sizing us up.

"He is this way." She turned and pushed the down button on a single elevator. It looked to be a service elevator, maybe used just for the jail.

"Have you worked here long?" I asked.

She nodded. "I'm Yona Watters."

CHAPTER 20

"YONA." TIMOTHY REACHED THROUGH the rusting bars and the two embraced as much as two people could through prison bars. They kissed. I stood flatfooted, not sure what to do or say.

"Are you okay? Did they hurt you?" Yona stepped back and looked Timothy over.

"I'm fine. They pushed me around a little, but nothing to worry about." The lights flickered. I looked around for cameras, but didn't see any.

"So … I take it you two know each other?" I said, breaking the moment. "Or is this how every prisoner is treated?"

Timothy smiled and looked around nervously. "Cameras?"

Yona shook her head. "Just at the main doors. We should be safe."

Joshua spoke up. "Miss Watters, what relation are you to Takota Watters?"

She squeezed Timothy's hand. "I'm his sister. Much younger sister. And I'm afraid that my relationship with Timothy makes this case a hundred times more complicated. My brother would like nothing more than to keep him behind bars."

From the way her voice trembled and the worry in her eyes, I could tell she was under a lot of stress.

I was feeling the stress too. So much to do, so little time. The longer he stayed here, the harder it would be to get him out of this situation and find the real killer. "Joshua, can you do me a favor?" I whispered. "Go see if you can find out where Lina Sever worked. I'll follow up with you after we're done here."

He nodded and turned toward the elevator at the far end of the hall.

"Can you unlock the door so we can talk a little easier?"

Yona shook her head. "I don't have a key, and unless we are in an interrogation room, they wouldn't approve of letting him out."

"They, meaning Chaska Tate and—"

"And me." Everyone jumped at the sound of a deep voice coming from the open elevator doors. I spun around, and Timothy and Yona pulled apart like two teenagers caught by a parent.

The very tall and very Indian man walked toward us with slow, confident strides. He wore a designer suit and had an expensive haircut—he had a white streak above each of his ears, and a scar on his lip. I wondered if he'd seen Yona and Timothy kissing. "I see you found the prisoner. I'm Takota Watters." He put out his hand and smiled as if he was about to ask me out to dinner.

"Sarah Steele." His hand was warm, and he shook mine with the perfect amount of firmness.

"Yes, I know. My head of security said you were beautiful. I see he still has a good eye for women." Turning to Yona, he frowned. "You can go now." She hung her head and hurried back down the hall.

I was about to make a jab at how he was being domineering toward his sister, but I wanted to gauge him better before I stepped into a hole I couldn't get out of.

"I'm going to take a wild guess and say that you are the FBI contact." I wondered how that ever got pushed through.

"You're smart, too. Impressive." His dark eyes searched mine and it made me uncomfortable. He was a stunning man, well built for his age, with amazing skin. "Yes, I work for the FBI as well as for the tribal council. And I own this casino." He chuckled. "Well, all three casinos."

Timothy grunted. "You treat everything as if you own it. Even your sister."

Watters shot Timothy an amused look. "Mr. James, I see you've got yourself into more trouble. I thought I warned you to keep out of things that were none of your business."

"The abuse of women going unpunished is my business. Or don't you care about your own family? Yona could be next!"

Watters didn't flinch. "I care a great deal, but you have your job and I have mine. Now, Miss Steele. You may talk to the prisoner, but do not touch him or get close enough to pass something to him. If you wish, I can have an interrogation room set up for you." He lifted an eyebrow and leaned closer to me. I could smell his aftershave, and it was not altogether unpleasant.

"That won't be necessary." I didn't want anyone listening in on our conversation.

"Very well. I wanted to meet you and let you know that as long as you respect our rules, you are welcome to visit Timothy during regular visiting hours."

"Thank you. And will you be in charge of the investigation?"

"I am, but there is not much to investigate." His eyes hardened. "We have our killer. You can start preparing for the trial. He'll be judged fairly for his crimes."

Anger welled up in me, but I choked it down. "We both know he didn't do it." I was having a hard time keeping my voice calm.

He put his hands behind his back. "You have your version—I have mine. We will work to get a trial date as soon as possible. People will want to see justice done."

Justice? What is that? "And if I can prove he didn't do it, what then?"

"I'm not interested in poking holes in this case, Miss Steele. If you come up with evidence, I will listen. But I will not be swayed by anything that points to some unknown killer. You produce a murderer, and I will free your man." He leaned down so he could look me in the eye. I wish I'd worn heels. "But I'd say your evidence is long gone. Don't waste your time."

With that, Watters turned and left the way he'd come. I stood staring after him and all at once felt completely helpless. He pushed the elevator call button and turned his head back down the hall. "Tick tock, Miss Steele. We don't like drawn-out trials like you white people do. Justice must be swift and sure. If you plan to prove your client's innocence, I suggest you get to it."

With that, the doors slid open and he stepped inside. I stood in stunned silence, not sure what to say or do next. There were times when I got stumped. Not many times, but I knew that, in a minute or two, I would think of a great comeback. Damn him.

I had to figure out who the real killer was before Timothy's trial. There were people to interview and evidence to collect—no time to waste feeling helpless.

I crossed my arms. "Don't get comfortable," I called to Timothy. "You won't be in this dungeon long."

He gripped his hair and closed his eyes. My heart wrenched in sympathy. "You've got to tell me more," I said. "Tell me anything, everything you know about this place and your work here."

Single bulbs hung down the center of the long hall and barred cells lined each side. There were maybe twenty holding cells in all, no windows, not much light, and it felt like the air wasn't moving at all.

"It doesn't look good, Timothy. They have their own rules here and you really must have pissed off some important people."

"Just wait till they read my story in the paper."

I stopped pacing. "Are you going to print it?"

"I have to. That or use it to force them to make some changes."

I shook my head. "No way. Your life is on the line."

He nodded and looked down at his feet. "I know, but you don't understand. What goes on around here—it's wrong. I have to tell the world about it, especially if I end up … well, if the worst should happen, it can't be at the expense of my silence. I have to get word to my editor."

I admired his courage, but wondered why he cared so much. "Why haven't you sent it in yet?"

Timothy rubbed his jaw and sighed. "Yona. She wants me to hold it, to wait until she talks to her brother and Chaska Tate. She wants to reason with them, talk to them and change what's been going on around here before I call them out. She has a lot at stake here too. She's written the U.S. government trying to get aid for the women's shelter program. She founded a shelter ten years ago and uses her own money to find housing for single mothers, abused women, and the like. She's convinced she can get through to them."

"Does she have any pull with Chaska?"

He nodded. "Yes, she's the only thing standing in the way of all-out war between the two. They both respect her, and at one time, Chaska was in love with her."

This surprised me a little. They both seemed to treat her like a slave, as if she were just some secretary. "Yeesh. She's so much younger than him."

"By at least twenty years. I don't know what happened, but I know if Chaska finds out that we are … that …"

"That you're in love with each other?"

Timothy blew out a shuddering breath. "They would kill me."

CHAPTER 21

AFTER AN HOUR OF talking with Timothy, I felt like I had a good handle on what he was working on and the nature of what I was getting myself into.

"The first issue is that the casinos are used to smuggle in drugs, women, and money. Everything is about the casinos," Timothy said. "They employ most of the tribe, they bring in a lot of money, and every member gets a fat check each month—bribe money to keep quiet about anything the powers tell them to keep quiet about. The second issue is the abuse of women in the tribe. There were more than fifty-two rapes in the past two years and only one man was ever incarcerated—and he had spent a whole sixty days behind bars before he got out on bail."

I typed notes in my phone as he spoke. The situation was bad, and I could see now that Timothy had stirred up a hornets' nest. "No wonder you were set up. You can make a lot of unwanted trouble for the tribe members if you go public."

"I know, but someone has to do something. Men from outside the reservation know that what happens here stays here. It's like a rape Vegas, and it brings in gamblers and lowlife from all over. The women aren't safe, and they're starting to stand up for themselves. That's why Yona was ready to work with me when I showed up to research my story."

"How did you hear about all this? I mean, what led you to your story idea?"

"I got a tip from a source—I can't say who, but it was good enough that I had to follow it up."

Standing, I stretched and looked up and down the hall to the poorly maintained jail.

"This is like the mob. Power, abuse, and corruption. Only problem is, they're their own nation and don't have to report anything. It's the perfect setup for organized crime."

Timothy agreed.

"Okay, I think I have enough for now. I need to talk with my partners and see what they found out. But I have a much better picture of what we're dealing with here."

After making my way up the elevator, I was about to leave the office when Yona came from behind her desk and took me aside. "Miss Steele," she said in a whisper. "Please be careful. I don't want you to end up like Timothy, or worse. He was asking the right questions of the wrong people and look what happened. It may be best if you let me handle it by myself."

"I'll be fine. Besides, I have you to look out for me." I was trying to lighten the mood, but she didn't crack a smile.

"I don't think you understand." Her eyes darted around like a scared child's.

"Why don't I stay with you for a day or so? That way, you can keep an eye on me and I won't get myself killed." I was hoping I could get her alone, and nothing makes a girl open up more than a night of wine and ice cream.

Yona looked at me and then over her shoulder as if she was

worried someone was eavesdropping. "That's not a good idea—you're an outsider. Just go home and don't stay here in the hotel, whatever you do."

"Yona, you're not alone anymore. I'm here, and I won't let anything happen to Timothy." She didn't seem reassured, but there was only so much I could do.

I texted Joshua and he said he still needed another hour. So I decided to jump in the car and explore the town—the real town, not this casino façade. After a five-minute drive down a two-lane highway, I pulled into a beautiful town square surrounded by boutiques and cute restaurants. A shabby little building sat in the corner with "Women's Clinic" on the awning. It looked out of place, like it was the only building no one cared about. There were walking paths through the square, a huge fountain in the middle, and little ponds lined with trees and beautifully landscaped lawns.

I picked up a sandwich from the café and took a walk around. There was a lot of money flowing through this place, and expensive cars were parked on the street.

It was warm, and I found a bench where I could wait for Joshua and people watch. He texted and said he was almost done. I finished my sandwich. It was getting close to dinnertime and I had to decide if I was going to stay here tonight or drive back to Boise.

Some boys were skateboarding up and down the square, hooting at any girl they passed. I rolled my eyes at the youthful mating calls. I guess it was the same no matter your blood background—boys were boys.

"You lost, white girl?"

I turned toward the voice and saw a man who looked to be in his twenties. He had two other guys with him, all with long hair and tribal tattoos.

"Nope, I know just where I am." I gave him a confident smile.

Far from being scared, I was aware of everything. If this guy wanted a fight, he'd picked the wrong girl.

"I don't think you do. You must be lost because you're sitting on our bench."

CHAPTER 22

THE THREE YOUNG MEN laughed and walked around me like sharks about to feed. "I think you should run along and find somewhere else to sit," one said, sneering at me.

I didn't think they were that dangerous, but as soon as they began taunting me I saw the group of skaters hurry over. From their gleeful expressions, I didn't think they'd come to help me.

"Look, I'm just sitting here eating a late lunch. I've had a hard day, and if you'll wait a few minutes, I'll be done and you can have your bench back." I was tired and my mind was going over the case backward and forward, beginning its overthinking craziness, so I knew I was in for a sleepless night to boot.

"But we want it now, don't we?" The ringleader waved a hand to the others and they nodded. I counted eight in the group. I was beginning to wonder if this bench was worth the fight to keep, which just pissed me off more.

"We don't like people like you around here—stinks up the place. The casino is crap-full of your kind—run back there. So if you don't mind . . . " He took my arm and began to lift me up.

My body flooded with electric energy. I spun toward him and kneed him in the groin as hard as I could. He let out a girlish moan and I came down on the back of his neck with an elbow. He hit the ground hard and everyone stood staring at me in shock.

"Now," I said lightly, barely panting. "Anyone else want this bench?"

If they did the math, they would see that no matter how strong I was, they had the numbers. But I was betting these guys weren't great at math. Just as one turned angrily to me, his hand raised, Yona came running into the middle of the circle.

"Boys, what are you doing?" When they saw her, their demeanor changed instantly. Their shoulders hunched and none of them would meet her eyes. She spoke in a motherly tone. "This is our guest. Why are you disrespecting her like this?" The group hung their heads, and one kid kicked the ground with his boot. I could tell that they knew her, even feared her—or maybe just feared her brother.

"We were just messing around, Yona," one of the boys said. "Meant no disrespect to you." Yona helped up the guy I'd kneed and he hobbled away.

"You should be kind to women, especially guests," Yona scolded them, and the group meandered off.

Yona turned to me and wagged a finger in my face. "I told you to be careful. What were you doing?"

"Trying to eat my lunch." I sipped from my water bottle and brushed the wrinkles out of my blouse.

Yona sighed and put her hands on her hips. "You can stay with me tonight, but only because you're trying to help Timothy."

I smiled. "Thank you so much. Got room for two?"

CHAPTER 23

YONA'S HOUSE WAS STYLISH and beautiful—designed with lots of natural light and dark wood trim, and her color palette was earthy and warm. I instantly felt relaxed, and the wine glass she handed me full of pinot noir helped me relax even further. We sipped as she gave me a tour. I stopped at a vintage photo, framed, that hung above her fireplace. It was of a young Indian woman with a tiny baby on her lap. Her big eyes sparkled as she held the child.

"Who's this?"

Yona's mouth pulled down in sadness. "That's my grandmother. She was an amazing woman, full of joy and love for her family, and the best at making fried pies in the whole town."

"Fried pies? That's a thing?"

"Yes." She smiled.

"I need one."

"We'll find you one tomorrow." She looked back up at the picture. "She died in childbirth. I hung it up there to remember. It gives me purpose."

"What do you mean?"

She looked back at me. "Gram could easily have survived if there'd been proper health care here. It's my goal to get every woman and child good health care and safe homes."

I nodded. "That's why you got involved with Timothy. He was going to bring about change."

Her cheeks grew rosy and they offset her smooth complexion. "I never knew it would end so badly for him."

I set my jaw. "Yona, you've got power here to stop this."

She shook her head, and her petite shoulders sagged. "I can't turn on my family. I know that Chaska and my brother seem horrible to you, but they didn't start out that way. They're legends for fighting for the rights of their people. A lot of us, including Chaska, were disappointed when Watters started casinos because we wanted to rise through other means. We have really gifted people in our tribe—writers and athletes and a young man who even won the state science fair last year. But Watters' business is pulling us down. There's a high rate of alcoholism and teen pregnancy and a low rate of college degrees, not to mention the horribly high rates of murder, drugs, rape, and sexual abuse." She sighed. "Chaska votes against the casinos every year, but Watters has a lot at stake. With the elections coming up, Watters will do anything to become chief so his beloved casinos will stay open. And Chaska is cornered."

"Cornered men are very dangerous."

"Exactly, and with the money the tribe makes off the casinos, he's swaying the vote."

She went on to explain some of the laws and cultural expectations surrounding a murder of one of their own. If they let Timothy go right now, it'd look like Chaska was catering to him—and if he started an investigation in the tribe, he'd be kicking an already-angry tribal council.

A crazy thought went through my mind. "Unless he killed her

himself."

"Sarah!" Her voice took on a chiding tone. "How could you think that? He's a respectable man."

"Right, sorry. But everyone's a suspect, and I have to follow the facts if we want to help Timothy and find out the truth." I took a gulp of wine. "Listen, thanks so much for talking, and for taking me in."

"I'll do anything to help Timothy. Or…" she amended, "almost anything."

"Then help me!" I tried to say as gently as possible, but my frustration must have shown through. "Please, how can I prove Timothy's innocence? Who has the most to lose if that story gets out?"

Her eyes widened. "I don't know, I swear. God, of course I don't know. But …"

"What?"

"You should talk to Mika and Skah at the Wild Wild West show. They know what goes on behind the closed casino doors that I don't. My brother tries to keep my hands clean." She took another sip. "But no one's clean. We're all guilty."

I was about to ask what she meant by that when she turned away. She showed me into my room, which was a nice, albeit simple, guest room. Then she softly said good night. She was done talking, and I wondered if I'd pushed her too far.

I gave a long, drawn-out sigh and closed my eyes. Yona talked as if she were powerless, and I wished she could find the strength within herself. At least she'd given me something to go on.

Just as soon as I flopped down on my bed, my phone buzzed. It was Solomon.

"Hey, babe, you home tonight or out hunting?" he said with a hint of humor in his voice.

I missed him, and even with everything going on right now, a part of me wanted to skip town with him and forget the world for a month or two. "I'm staying at the reservation. Don't worry, I'm okay."

"You're hard not to worry about. Trouble seems to like you."

"Tell me about it. That's why you like me—because I'm trouble." I laid my head back on the pillow.

"Maybe. I like a little adventure in my life." He was flirting, and I changed the subject.

"I sent Joshua home. I don't really need a car around here, and he has to work tomorrow."

"Why do you do that? When I try to flirt, make a sexual joke, or just tease you, I get the cold shoulder," Solomon said, tension lacing his voice.

"I'm sorry. I'm just in the middle of this case and my mind isn't, you know, in the mood."

"Sarah, you started it. You made a joke, and this isn't the first time. I thought we had something here, that you and I were official and working toward something …"

He let his voice fade, and I hated myself for doing this to him. I wanted to be close, but it was so hard. Why did I shut down and push him away? I knew I did it, but I didn't know how to stop.

"I'm sorry, Solomon. I could give you a million reasons why, but they're just excuses." I wanted to cry but held it back, pushed it away like I did with so many people in my life.

There was silence on the other end and I wondered if he would end it with me right here and now on the phone. "Sarah." His tone was soft, forgiving. "I care about you, I want to be with you, but you have to let me in. Quit pushing me away. I can take a lot, but the one thing I can't take is being pushed away."

"I know."

"I like you and your sexy legs, your sweet smile, and the way you kick butt in and out of the courtroom. You are the perfect mix of badass and sweet sugar."

"Now who's starting it?"

"Okay, okay, I'll stop being a sap bucket." Changing gears, he grunted and cleared his throat. "So are you making any headway on the case?"

My insides melted and relaxed all at the same time. Solomon knew how to push me, and sometimes he knew exactly what I needed. And right now it was to stay focused and to put him and our relationship problems on hold.

CHAPTER 24

I RATTLED ON ABOUT the case, and Solomon listened and said yes and no and hmm in all the right places. "Joshua found out that Lina Sever was a cocktail waitress at the Golden Nugget. I'm going to run down some leads, see if there's any connection between the murder and past killings."

"How many have there been?"

"Five, maybe more. And that's just in the past year."

Solomon whistled. "And you say there's going to be an election?"

"Yeah, a big one. If Chaska loses his seat, his whole family could be kicked out of the tribe one way or another. If that happens, it's going to get ugly. Chaska won't go down without a fight."

On the ride out to her house, Yona had told me that people were getting tribal council letters bringing their blood heritage into question. They demanded proof of tribal membership by a blood test or direct birth line.

"It's like this twisted power play, with so many different angles to look at. I think Timothy James just happened to get mixed up with the wrong tribe at the wrong time."

"So what are you going to do?"

I was wondering the same thing myself. Without finding the real killer, I would never get Timothy out of jail. And to make matters worse, nothing about the murder was public. There was a local paper, and so far, nothing had been said about it. They were working hard to keep it under wraps. "I don't know. I have to find the real killer, but I'm scared that it's someone they'll fight to protect. Either Chaska or Watters knows who it is already. Heck, maybe both of them do."

"Let me know if there's anything I can do on my end. I'll help out as much as I can."

"Thanks, I will. So, I need something nice to think of while I go to sleep." I smiled and hoped that our little spat didn't put him off too much. "What are you wearing?"

Solomon laughed and lowered his voice. "Just a smile, babe, just a smile."

After we were done talking, I hung up and got into my pajamas— aka yoga pants and tank top—and cozied up under the plush comforter and downy pillow, and then it happened. My insomnia woke up. It'd plagued me ever since the Williams case and it was beginning to get on my nerves. With a huff, I got out of bed and went to the kitchen to get a glass of milk so I could down two melatonin pills.

The house was insanely nice. Wood beams throughout every room, tall windows looking out to the desert and stone accents around the fireplace and in the kitchen. Distracted, I walked from room to room and did the math, guessing the house was around fifteen thousand square feet.

Yona lived alone and drove a black BMW. The casino was paying all the tribe members really well. And even if they had to live out in the middle of nowhere, they did it in style.

I found a Key lime pie in the subzero double-door fridge and took a slice to go. It was just what I needed—a little cold and sweet mixed with the perfect amount of sour.

Wandering from the kitchen, I found myself in a long hall with floor-to-ceiling windows on one side overlooking a pool. It was blue and illuminated by small lights placed in the landscaping around the outdoor oasis. Not bad—palm trees and everything.

The feeling of being on some other world washed over me. It was like this place—the casinos, the way everything was set up—was just not right, as if it was a kids' playhouse in the courtyard of a maximum security prison. But here it was, in all its glory—its lonely, sad glory.

All the way in the back of the house and down a flight of stairs was a full basement and game room. Pool table, big movie screen, and even an old-school arcade game, The Lone Ranger. I liked her style.

Everything smelled new and unlived in. I wondered if she ever used half this stuff, ever had parties or people over. Somehow I doubted it. I had expected her to live a little less extravagantly with how much she gave to the shelter. Something was not right, not right at all.

I was about to go back upstairs when I saw a wooden door almost hidden in the corner. I assumed it was storage or something like that, but it was placed wrong. Yona's office?

Pushing the door open, I saw a cluttered desk with books all over it, like a used bookstore blew up and it all landed in this room. Now this was more like it—this room was used.

Flipping on the light, I shut the door behind me and sat in the big well-worn chair and ate the last bite of Key lime pie.

Yona's office was not huge like the rest of her house. It was dimly lit, with stacks of books on the floor, all over the desk, and bookcases around the room stuffed with paperbacks and papers. There was just enough room for the door to open and the chair to move around on its little plastic floor pad.

Pictures tacked to the walls showed Yona and much younger versions of Chaska Tate and Watters. In the pictures was the sad story.

Smiles, Yona holding a fishing pole, and Chaska kissing her on the cheek. Watters and Chaska sitting on a log eating their lunch. Even though Chaska was at least ten years older than Watters, it was clear they were best friends at one time.

What happened to them? How could they go from being three best friends to enemies?

I flipped through old photo albums and saw more of the same. The bottom drawer of the old desk was locked, but I worked it with a bobby pin. Inside was a box covered with soft pink flowers. It was coming apart at the seams, and inside were letters. Love letters.

I felt bad looking through them, but they put more of the story into focus. Yona and Chaska were lovers. He told her he wanted to marry her. Once she was old enough and her brother was back from college, they would set a date. Chaska wanted Watters to be his best man.

Finding the envelope with the most recent date, I read the last letter Chaska wrote to Yona.

Dear Yona,

My love, my heartbreak, my pain. All I ever wanted was you. All I ever dreamed of was you and the life we could have as one. But you have betrayed me, left me for him, to take the side of your traitor brother over the man who has given up everything for you.

Why?

I see you and my heart is torn open all over again. I remember holding you in my arms, kissing you, loving you, and now you won't even look at me.

Can't you see what he is doing? He wants the casinos, is hungry for money and filled with greed. That school, the one I paid for, has turned him against us. Yes, we are all making more money, but at what cost? At the cost of our love?

I will not fight him. I love you too much. Let this act be the proof of how I feel. I will give Watters the casinos. He can have them, make them into what he wants, and I won't stand in his way.

I do this for you. You mean more than any amount of money, more than any earthly possession. Come back to me, love me like you did once before the poison of bitterness swept over your soul.

I will never give up on us. I will always love you even if from a distance.

Yours always and forever,

Chaska

I folded the letter back into its faded envelope and put the box away. My heart felt heavy and I could see now that all this was because of two lovers who had to choose between love or family.

Some say blood is thicker than water, but I never believed that—sometimes blood was just blood.

CHAPTER 25

THE NEXT DAY, I decided to wear something a bit more salacious. I wore a skirt, black leggings, and a V-neck top. A hint of my cleavage popped out, and when I slipped into my red heels, it completed the transformation. Now I looked like I would fit in at the casino if I were there to gamble.

After a simple breakfast of eggs and toast and rich coffee, Yona took me to the Golden Nugget, where the Wild Wild West show was. She said she was going to visit Timothy. I gave her my number and wished her luck.

I easily found the theater, as signs were plastered for it all over the place. The cowgirl in the photo was cute, and looked to be about sixteen years old. The man in the picture had war paint and leather buckskin pants, pulling back a bow. There was a scar on his forehead. He was handsome, but had the body of a boy, not a man. Something about him made me uneasy.

The theater held at least five hundred people with stadium seating, and up front was a VIP section. There were even box seats up top, and I could only imagine the ticket price.

Walking with an air of confidence and hoping no one noticed I didn't belong, I made my way backstage. It was total chaos, with horses and carriages and more weapons than I'd seen in ten years in the city. It smelled like a strange mixture of horses and hairspray. I asked around for someone named Mika.

A young man who wore a tight leather shirt and looked as out of place here as I felt as he held a shiny bay gelding motioned down the hall. "She's in her office—down the hall and second door on the left." I thanked him and found a small office marked "Director".

"Mika?" I peered in and saw a middle-aged woman with black-and-silver hair bent over some papers. "I'm Sarah Steele, assistant distri—" I caught myself. "I mean, I'm here because of Lina Sever."

Mika slumped in her chair. Her eyebrows creased and a deep sadness washed over her face. "What of Lina?"

I sat in a dusty folding chair and put my elbows on my knees, leaning forward. "I am trying to save a man's life and find the real killer, but it's very important that you tell me everything you know about Lina. I know you're a strong woman and can help me see this through until the end."

Her bottom lip trembled and she bit down on it as if to cover up how she felt inside. "Are you that lawyer everyone is all worked up about?"

I folded my hands in my lap. "Yes, and Yona said you were a good woman. You're the one who wrote The Horse Herder, didn't you? And won several awards for it."

Something flashed in her face—was it guilt? Or shame? "I'm a long way from the college girl who wrote that."

"You're who you choose to be," I said with a little smile. "Now, can you tell me who would gain if they harmed Lina?"

She sat for a moment, picking at her nails. Music blasted from the stage, muted by the door. Finally she said, "We not only have to find out who killed Lina—we have to find out who had Lina killed."

"And who framed Timothy James for it."

She sighed. "That poor reporter. He had no clue what he got into. And Lina—foolish girl with her foolish tongue. Talking about things that she should've kept quiet."

I felt like she was going to be one of my best allies if only I could get her talking. "So Lina was collateral damage?"

Mika put her face in her hands and wouldn't respond.

"Who'd be worst off if Timothy published his piece?"

Mika appeared stressed and shook her head. "I can't talk about this right now, not to you." Her eyes grew wide and her right hand shook, so she shoved it in her lap.

Why was she so afraid right now? She glanced down at her desk, and I wondered if maybe someone had bugged the place or monitored her here. I nodded, not wanting to push her or get her into trouble. "You know, when I'm stressed, I like to work out. Pound away on a heavy bag or go running to burn it off. Do you like to run, Mika?"

She swallowed and then nodded.

"I was thinking of going this evening. You could join me if you like. Eight o'clock? At the lovely little hiking trail south of town?"

She nodded again. I stood and held out my hand. "I'm going to watch your play later today."

"Oh, please don't." She flushed. "It's terrible. Completely trash."

I winked at her. "But the masses love it." I sighed. "The show must go on, huh?"

"Yeah, the show must go on."

A young girl with a clipboard came from another room in the back, passing racks of costumes. She smiled at me, then said to Mika, "They need you upstairs. Hotah got hammered and punched a guard. They need you to check to see if he's still able to go on stage."

Fire lit Mika's eyes and she stood and stomped out of her office.

"I'll deal with him."

"Be careful!" the girl called after her.

Mika stopped and took note of me. "Skah, please show Sarah around and get her a good seat for the two o'clock. I have to go see if our star is going on stage or to bed." She stormed off, muttering something about babysitting.

Skah smiled. She was a cute college-age girl with glasses and a small mouth. "Come with me. We're running late and our actors are divas today, but you're welcome to spy on us if you like. "

"How'd you know about my secret identity?" I smiled.

"Oh, everyone knows about you by now, Sarah Steele."

CHAPTER 26

IT WAS A RUSH, like the first time he picked up a bow at his grandmother's prodding. He took to it at once, became the best shot in the tribe, and traveled to archery competitions all over the States.

Now he stood, arms out as the crowd cheered. Smiles and nods of approval filled him with so much delight. The first act was his favorite—shooting a fire arrow through a hoop into a target. The crowd cheered at everything he did. The feeling of control filled him with such joy that he couldn't hold back a proud grin. Hotah bowed and left the stage, wondering what his dad would think of him now. He was sure he was off somewhere living the life, making love with celebrities, making millions. Or maybe he was a spy, like James Bond. He'd never met his father, but he knew he was a great man, nothing like his whore of a mother.

He threw open the door to his dressing room and placed his bow in a large safe. It was the most important thing in his life. Sometimes he felt like it was magical, the way it made his arrows fly true no matter what. He ran his fingers over the handmade arrows in his quiver. He'd made every one himself. Though his patience was short with everything else, he felt peace when he sat down in his wood shed and made arrows. It was an art. His grandmother taught him that by doing so, magic connected the maker with the arrow. He didn't believe it at first, but now he did.

Closing the safe, he took off his costume and began wiping off the war paint. His chest was hairless and smooth. He was never in to working out, so his body was not well muscled like some of the other guys his age. But he knew that the real power was in the will, the gut. And his gut was strong.

He heard someone go in the next dressing room and his heart sped up. He deserved a reward, something to celebrate his success. Going out into the hallway, he barged into the next room. In front of the mirror was Mika's little intern. What was her name? Skal? Skah? Whoever she was, she looked delicious.

"Hey, babe, good show, huh?" He ran a hand down the center of his own chest.

Skah turned and stared at him in disgust. "This is not your dressing room and I'm not your babe."

Hotah walked in and slid his arm around her waist. She smelled like lavender, making him want her. Skah twisted away and Hotah laughed. He'd always thought Skah was hot, though a little young for him. But her body wanted him—he could read the signs.

"Get out." Her voice shook, and he could see how scared she was of him. Now he wanted her even more. Taking a step forward, he reached for her, but she dodged and pushed him.

"If you touch me, I'll tell Watters."

Hotah snorted. "He said that I had his blessing. We're supposed to get married this spring. Didn't you hear? I just want to know what I'm getting. You know how it is—give the old horse a test drive."

Her face fell—or did it brighten? "You pathetic liar." She spat. Hotah started to unbuckle his belt, and she ran. He stood there in her dressing room shocked and confused. Why would she do that? He gritted his teeth and walked into the hall. Two dancers were coming his way. He slid his knife out of its holster and forced them into Skah's dressing room.

He wanted dessert and he was going to get it one way or another.

CHAPTER 27

I SPENT HALF THE day sniffing around the Golden Nugget, asking about Lina Sever. Her mother was a housekeeper at the hotel, but hadn't come to work that day. When I called her, I couldn't hear much past the sobbing and the accusations that Watters didn't keep any of his waitresses safe. Then she told me that Timothy needed to rot in hell and hung up. I spent a little time with one of Lina's friends, who told me more about her than I expected. She was broken-hearted and wanted a shoulder to cry on, which I provided. I learned that Lina dreamed about becoming a home designer and was taking classes online. She'd had a boyfriend who she broke up with, but he'd moved away shortly after that. Her friend had no idea why anyone would want to kill her.

I spend the rest of the day going through my e-mail. Joshua sent over a ton of information and most of it was on tribal law. At the end of the day, I had a lot of little puzzle pieces in my mind, but no clue how I'd put them together.

Frustrated and sore from sitting on hard chairs, I stood up and stretched. Maybe it was time to find some supper and catch up with

Mandy.

My phone buzzed. "Sarah, Sarah," Yona yelled on the other end of the line. I pulled the receiver from my ear, afraid she'd burst my eardrum. She sounded desperate, and scared.

"What?"

"Meet me in the Golden Nugget parking lot. Now!" Then she hung up.

I rushed down the hall and met her in the circular drive. She'd already pulled up to the doors. I jumped in and she sped off, tires screeching. "What is it?"

"Just wait." She ground her teeth and wiped tears from her cheeks. Horrible scenarios flew through my mind, but I knew better than to ask. "They're meeting us at my house."

"Who is?"

But she clammed up again.

When we got to her house, she ran through the doorway, me shadowing her. Mika and Skah were pacing in front of a large stone island.

"Mika, what's going on? Are you okay?" I asked, trying to keep my voice steady.

Skah spoke up, her voice cracking as she wiped her face with the back of her hand. "He killed them—there was blood everywhere. Why did he have to kill them?" She shook her head and looked at me as if I had the answer.

"Who? What happened?" I pulled out a bar stool and made the smaller of the two girls sit. Yona poured water in a kettle and took out a box of loose-leaf tea.

"Start over so Miss Steele can hear the whole story," Yona said. "She is Skah, and that's Mika." She motioned to them.

"Yes, we've met," I said. Skah cried in silence for a moment before Mika took her in her arms. I dreaded the story she was going to tell me.

Skah took the mug of hot tea Yona handed her and drew in a few labored breaths. "It's Hotah. He came in—"

"Did he touch you?" I interrupted, livid.

"No. He tried to goad me. You know him—he's always trying to get girls to sleep with him, but we all think he's a creep."

"He is a creep," Mika mumbled. Yona handed her a cup and one to me. I took it and wrapped my cool hands around the rim, glad for its heat.

"So he made a move on me. I'd seen him gawking at me the last few weeks and knew it would happen sooner or later, but he was drunk and being a total jerk."

The phone started ringing and Yona glanced at me, but didn't make a move to answer it.

"I tried to throw him out, but he wouldn't go, so I ran. I was lucky…" Skah choked up again and put her head in her hands. "He killed them."

Mika took over, holding Skah's hand. "Skah found me and we went back to her dressing room together. We found them—dead. There were two of them. One had an arrow in her chest, and the other looked like her head was almost cut off." Mika clenched her jaw, and I could see the anger boiling just under the surface. This was Lina all over again.

"Did you call the police?" I said.

Mika shook her head. "No. I went to Watters, and the casino security took over. They told us to keep quiet until they figured out what to do."

"What to do?" I exploded. "It's simple! Call the police!"

This time Yona spoke up. She'd been quiet the whole conversation, but I saw how upset she was now. "They will just cover it up. Two girls are dead—how many more are going to die before we do something?"

How could they not see that if they wanted change, they'd have to do it? "Mika! Remember when you wrote about love and justice?"

She nodded miserably. "Now I'm writing cheesy lines pitting Injuns against the white men. I hate it."

"Than change it!" I was about to spout out a Gandhi quote, but figured it'd be too much. "Could it be much worse? One out of three girls gets raped . . ."

Yona turned sharply. "Not by our men. It's psychos from every state within five hundred miles who know they can get away with anything here. The Justice Department never prosecutes."

Skah chimed in. "Only one man has been convicted of rape in the past three years, and he got off on parole. We don't even have the money at the women's shelter to buy rape kits anymore. That's why we had to—" She cut herself off, suddenly embarrassed. What's going on?

I raised my eyebrows. "That's true, but it's one of your own who's murdering. And we've got to stop him. What are you willing to do to change things here?"

They looked at each other, making a silent agreement. "Anything," they said.

The phone rang again and Yona finally answered it. She fell silent and then said "yes," "no," "yes," "yes," and hung up.

"An emergency council meeting has been called. I have to go." She stood.

"I'm going with you," I said.

Yona shook her head.

Skah and Mika stood and said in unison, "Us too."

CHAPTER 28

YONA TRIED TO KEEP Mika, Skah, and me from going, but we were having none of it. We all got in her car and she took off.

We were almost back in town when Yona made a turn on a dirt road and started heading the other way. I looked out at the lights in the distance and wondered where this council met. As if reading my mind, Mika touched me on the shoulder.

"The council likes to meet out away from everything. It's part of the old ways. Under the stars, back to our roots. It brings peace."

"Yona?" I asked. "Can Skah and Mika go into the meeting as witnesses? Skah's story could help prove that Hotah was at the scene of the crime."

Yona nodded. The dust made a cloud behind us and I smelled it through the car window. "They will accept them as witnesses, but they may not listen to them. We'll have to see."

I coughed. "But there's no way they're going to let me in, so I think I have an idea." I'd been racking my brain the whole ride over, trying to scheme a way into the council meeting. "Skah, do you have a phone? I don't have mine on me."

"Yeah." She pulled out a new iPhone. "Why?"

I took it, checked the battery, and sighed. It had only 15% power left. "Yona do you have a cell phone?"

Yona shook her head. "I left it at the house."

"Blast." Mika's phone had 50% so hers would be good, but the iPhone was going to be a problem. I hit the power button and closed out all the open programs in the hopes of conserving juice.

"What are you doing?" Mika asked.

"Getting me into the council meeting." I handed her phone back and said, "I'll call you once we get there. Put me on mute and put the phone in your pocket. I'll listen in with this phone. All you have to do is try to speak up and get as close to the action as you can. You think you can do that?"

Mika nodded.

"Good. Now let's just hope the battery holds out."

CHAPTER 29

I HIT SEND AND connected with Mika. All three girls were walking up to a stone archway into a huge building. The moon was big and cast long shadows over the landscape. I snuck around to the side and made my way up a small rise. I found a small outcropping that had a good view of the meeting below.

Yona walked through the archway and into the middle of an open square. Broken stone walls surrounded the square and a few side rooms were still intact. A fire burned in the middle and I counted twelve people, including Yona.

"Yona, glad you could make it. Please sit." The voice was clear—I thought it sounded like Watters. From my vantage point, I couldn't make out faces, but I could guess who was who.

Watters wore a headdress and a dark suit. He hugged Yona, and I could feel the tension from here.

"This has to stop, Watters. We have to do…" Her voice trailed off, and a young man without a shirt stood up. The firelight cast an eerie light across his bare chest. His body was one of a teen boy.

"What is he doing here?" Yona asked. Behind her, Skah

straightened up.

Chaska stood. "He's my apprentice, as I see you've brought yours." He motioned to Skah and Mika. The young man winked at Skah, and I knew it was Hotah.

"We are all here. Everyone, please sit, and the council meeting will come to order." Chaska sat at the top of the circle, and Yona and the girls found a spot and sat on the ground like the rest of the council.

Drums resounded through the small building.

"That is Hotah," Yona whispered so I could hear it. "He is here to mock us, to rub it in. He thinks he is invincible."

I looked down at the phone I held and saw that the battery was at 12%. I cursed.

The drumming abruptly ended and there came a chant that I heard up the hill. The meeting was getting underway and I was nervous. Or I should have been, but that dark thing inside was more excited than nervous.

CHAPTER 30

"THEY'RE LYING!" HOTAH WAS on his feet again, screaming at Skah and Mika. "Skah has tried to get me into bed a few times, and I turned her down! She wants what she can't have and it drives her crazy."

"You bastard." Skah lunged toward Hotah, and he spread his arms and laughed. "You would have raped me if I hadn't gotten away."

"So you say, whore."

Chaska held up his hand, and Tahatan moved as if to strike. The big man was wound tight. "Enough. This is childish. We have heard your testimony, and I am heartbroken about the events of this night. There are two dead because of this tragedy, and it has put our whole tribe is at risk. The last thing we need is for the outside to come in and mess with what we have worked so hard for."

Yona stood and spoke up. "Hotah is out of control. We all know he's Watters' lapdog, killing at his command. Watters needs to get him back on a leash. This feud is over—it ends tonight. I am sick of all the fighting, the killing—when will it end? When will it be enough?"

Watters sat in silence as if the council meeting was a sports game and he was a half-interested fan. When he stood, Yona sat, and everyone looked toward him. A calming mood fell over the council. "I have sat in many council meetings. My family has been a part of this tribe from the beginning. I was once a proud member. I saw my bloodline as a blessing, but now it is a curse. All I hear is accusations, lies, and stories."

Grinding my teeth, I fought my rising anger. The council members shot fearful looks at each other and the mood of the meeting turned. Yona and Chaska were the only ones who seemed immune to the trance Watters managed to put on the rest of the council. True power was not in money, but in what people thought of you. Even if it was a created illusion, Watters knew his people well, and just what to say to get them to bend to his will.

"We have a scorned woman lashing out at our own Hotah. Did anyone see him attack Skah? Did anyone see Hotah kill those women? No. The fact is that we have a murderer on the loose and all this meeting is doing is wasting time. As we fight and bicker, there is a killer out there, maybe killing again right now."

Chaska held up his hand and Watters sat. "I agree with Yona—this feud needs to end. I do not want to have more bad blood between us. This, as you know, Watters, has cost us much. But you have to face the truth—you have to be happy without control of the council."

"We shall see, brother," Watters said with a dismissive wave of his hand.

Chaska leaped to his feet in a rage and Tahatan reached to stop him. I was already on my feet and running. The council meeting was not going to get past the families' blood feud, meaning a killer was going to walk free. That was something I couldn't sit by and watch.

CHAPTER 31

THE CONTROL OVER MY inner monster was still there, in place and strong. But I just didn't care anymore. Dodging sagebrush and rocks, I vaulted a low part on the broken wall and shot through the archway. The council members turned to stare at the crazy white woman who had just busted in on their meeting.

"This is ridiculous," I shouted. "You have the killer right here." I pointed to Hotah and he lifted his head, smiling.

Skah and Yona were huddled together, scared, but Mika had a fire in her eyes, like she was cheering me on. Two other men I had never seen before held Chaska back. "What's the meaning of this, Miss Steele? How dare you come into the council? This is an affront to—"

I crossed my arms. "Skah was assaulted by him today, and an hour later two girls are found dead in her dressing room. What more proof do you need? Hotah's arrows stopped the hearts of two girls. Don't you think he should be the first suspect?"

Hotah jumped up. "They were stolen from me! Anyone can walk into my changing room. People out there are jealous of me, and this is a clear setup to ruin my good name."

"Liar." I marched to stand beside Tahatan, pointing at the people in a circle. "And whoever hired him needs to be his cell mate."

Tahatan swore and grabbed my arm, spinning me around. He pulled me close and growled in my ear. "Watch yourself. Steele. There's only so much I can do to protect you."

This threw me. I saw the man as an enemy. Why would he warn me? "Let me go." I could feel my own heartbeat where his hand gripped my arm.

"Tahatan, I demand you arrest this woman," Watters said in a voice that rang throughout the room. "She is an outsider and is trespassing on sacred ground." Watters lost his stone-like countenance. Hotah sat to his left and had a huge smirk on his face.

"Arrest me? Really?" For a wild minute, I considered fighting Hotah right there, right then, and seeing who would come out alive. "But you have the real killer sitting right behind you. Arrest him and let Timothy go. It's clear he's not the killer."

Watters took three steps forward and backhanded me across the face. Hot tears rushed to my eyes. I yanked free of Tahatan's grasp and hit Watters in the throat with the palm of my hand.

Someone yelled, and it sounded like I was about to be run down by a stampede of cattle. I turned to see Yona pushing past a tall man, trying to reach me. He threw her to the ground.

Watters yanked my hair, and I hit the broken concrete hard. My knees burned. A palm to the throat would put most men down, but he acted like I had only slapped him.

A hand hauled me up and I struggled to get free. I saw Watters in front of me, and he was in a defense stance. I kicked him in the balls. He buckled and went down. I smiled in spite of myself and pain shot from my neck down my left arm … Then my world went black.

CHAPTER 32

THE DECREPIT CABIN SAT at the end of a long driveway, hidden by trees. The sun set in glorious hues of red and orange, and the stars began twinkling on the horizon. Thick forests teeming with birds and wildlife surrounded the little road. Hotah had spent his boyhood hunting in those woods. His grandma had come to depend on the rabbits and deer meat he'd bring home for supper. It was his getaway, his safe place.

That's why he'd asked to meet his employer here. On his territory.

Hotah put his feet up on a wooden desk and shoved a stack of papers onto the floor. They were in his way, and he didn't like things to be in his way.

"You think this is funny? Some sort of joke?" Chaska poured a glass of Jack for himself and downed it on one gulp. "How did she find out you were hired to kill that girl?"

Hotah grinned. "Who cares? She thinks I work for Watters, so let it ride. Besides, she hit him. Charge her for assault and let her rot. I could play with her in jail and she'd regret ever speaking out against us."

Chaska slammed the glass down and glared at Hotah. "You are

missing the point. She knows too much, and is learning more every day. By tomorrow, she could have our list of suppliers! Who knows what she would come up with by the end of the week. How am I supposed to protect the tribe if I lose the council? All I need is some outsider snooping around, making trouble."

"Let me kill her. That'd fix it."

"No. You are done killing. You killed two showgirls? What's wrong with you?"

"It would have been fine if that Steele woman hadn't butted in. She is a problem and I deal with problems, remember?"

"Yeah, but she did butt in, and now we have to lay low. You are finished."

Hotah stood up, took the glass from Chaska, and poured from a bottle of Jack. He sipped it casually. "I don't think so. I've been your errand boy for far too long and what this tribe needs is leadership, which you are lacking." Before Chaska could react, Hotah brought the half-empty bottle around and hit Chaska across the side of the face, splitting his ear open. Blood leaked out of a large gash and Chaska wobbled.

"Sit, old man."

Chaska fell into his chair, and Hotah kicked the door shut and locked it. This was going to be more fun than the girls. Taking out his hunting knife, he walked around to the big man and grabbed his hand.

"Try not to struggle. I might accidentally cut off two fingers instead of just one."

CHAPTER 33

MY HEAD POUNDED AND my eyes stung. I blinked a few times before I realized where I was.

Jail.

Timothy was in the next cell over, and he smiled at me through the bars as I sat up.

"I see you've been making some progress in the case."

"Ha, funny. I think all I did was show my hand." I rubbed the back of my neck and winced when my hand touched the lump. That was going to leave a nasty bruise. "I think I made an impression on Watters. He'll be walking a little bowlegged for a few days." The place smelled like mold and dust, making my nose itch. I slowly sat upright on the metal cot with a skanky blanket at its foot. When was the last time it had been washed?

I filled Timothy in on the information I found at Yona's house. He took it all in and said, "Maybe that's why I am in here, half because what I found out about the tribe and the other half because of Yona. Chaska was in love with her—still is, from the sound of it, and she and I . . ." His voice trailed off.

"Do you love her?"

Timothy nodded. "I never intended for it to happen. She was helping me. She really believes there can be peace between Chaska and Watters. I don't know if it will ever happen—so much blood has been spilt."

I tried to put it all together in my mind. "So Chaska is in love with Yona. Watters was sent to business school on Chaska's dime and comes back to run the casinos, but then takes them over. Chaska has the council and Watters has the money, controls people through their living, and if they step out of line, he calls their blood rights up for question."

"Something like that, and don't forget the drugs, prostitution, and who knows what else. There are dirty hands on both sides. It makes me want to get out of here and forget this ever happened." Timothy sighed and hung his head.

"And let them get away with murder? Look how many are dead. It's not the council that's suffering—it's the people. Yeah, they get loads of money, but it's all a sham, a way to control them, and if they mess up or fight back, they're killed. This has to stop, and you and I are the only ones who have any ability to do it. But first, we have to get out of here."

"How do you propose we do that?"

Before I could answer, the elevator at the end of the hall opened and light flooded in. The shadow of a man crept along the floor, and a second later, Hotah stood staring at the two of us as if we were monkeys in a zoo.

"Well, well, well. The two troublemakers."

"What do you want, Hotah?" I spit out his name as if it tasted bad.

"We've never been introduced, not officially. I'm your god, and you've angered me."

Timothy sat still and I laughed. "Ha. If you're God, then I'm Elvis come back from the dead." I knew I shouldn't mock him, but he was so arrogant, and I couldn't believe he believed his own crap. I bet he drove a jacked-up 4X4 and popped his collar.

"Laugh all you want." He pulled something out of his pocket. Was it a pale cigar? "But I'm out here and you are in there. If you still think you're in control of things that happen around here, you're as dumb as you look."

"Something I shall soon remedy." I stood up and sauntered over to him. "You might not be so confident if I were on the other side of these bars."

This time he laughed. "You're funny. Maybe I'll do you like I did the others." He tossed the object at me. I caught it as it tumbled down my shirt, leaving a little red trail. Was that a—? I screamed and lurched back, dropping it on the floor.

It was a human finger.

CHAPTER 34

"WE'VE GOT TO GET out of here," Timothy said.

"It would seem like a good idea." We were once again alone. I'd thrown the finger out of the cell, but could still see it from the corner of my eye. "Do you think Yona or Mika will help us?"

Timothy sighed. "I'm not sure. Yona loves her people, but hates what is going on. Did I ever tell you about the book Mika wrote?"

"I've heard of it. Do you think it can help us?"

"It's all about a fictional tribe and the abuse of women, greed, and well, it's about this place, but with different names and locations. It did really well and even won some book awards. She used the money to start a woman's rescue shelter with Yona. It's a small building outside of town. It was there before the casinos went big. Now no one is in need of money."

"Didn't the book anger the tribe? They had to know it was about them."

"Yeah, but it was fictional. I suspect Chaska had something to do with the fact that she wasn't shunned for it. He has a blind eye when it comes to her."

I sat down on the edge of the metal bed and rubbed my temples. I had to get a hold of Joshua, Solomon, and Mandy. This was not looking good.

"You think I can get them to give me my phone call?"

"What do you want to do, order a pizza?" Timothy said. My stomach rumbled, and I didn't think that was a half- bad idea.

"Yeah, with a key mixed in the tomato sauce."

Hours passed, and Timothy and I were no closer to finding a way out. For the first time, I was starting to get worried about my own safety. I knew that if it went a few days, Solomon would come looking, but in that time, they could have us killed and buried out in the desert somewhere.

My eyes were getting heavy and I had a headache. I lay down and tried to think. The last time I'd felt this helpless was when my father died. I know how bad it is to stuff feelings, but sometimes what is good for the mind is bad for the soul.

The elevator bell dinged and Timothy and I both jumped. The click of heels on concrete made me tense up. I smelled coffee and cigarettes. Was it Hotah again?

Watters stepped into the light. He had two cups and was dressed in jeans and a nice button-up shirt. He handed me one of the cups and I almost hugged it. Never had coffee tasted so good. Why was he being nice, and what did he want?

"I'm sorry," he said.

I nodded and took a sip of my drink. It would take a lot more than an apology and coffee to fix what he'd broken, but it was a start.

His eyes were sad. "I know what you must think of me, but I've had some time to mull things over. In the council meeting, Yona said something that bothered me."

It was hard to look him in the eye when the last time I saw him, he'd backhanded me. But I tried. He was my only chance out. "Oh, so you listen to women after all?"

He ignored my comment.

"She accused me of hiring Hotah. As if he was my henchman or something."

"You claimed him."

"No, Miss Steele. I trained him for the show, and I hoped he would go to college like I did and get away from the tribe. But her accusation got me thinking. If she knew that he was hired and it wasn't me, it must have been Chaska. Now before you speak or makeup your mind, please hear me out."

I took another sip of my coffee. Timothy listened in from the next cell, leaning toward us. From the corner of my eye, I could see him trying not to draw attention to himself.

"This feud started out small—just some hurt feelings—and now it's out of control. I take ownership of my part, but I've never killed anyone or hired anyone to kill for me. Yes, I have fought back and called into question some of the members' bloodlines as a way to get the tribe split and see it my way. I even have used money and the casino jobs as a way to control them. I see now that it was wrong, and I plan to end it. The most important thing is that we fix what is wrong in the tribe, not go to war over who sits as chief."

If my jaw could have hit the floor, it would have. This was unexpected and a little strange. I didn't trust him. "Why now? What brought on this change of heart?"

Watters sighed. "My sister Yona. She is a noble woman and good at protecting the girls in the village. They need it. But now, even she is not able to save them. Like her, I do not want to see more people hurt. But I am in bed, as you may say, with some bad people. Changing things will take some time, and it could cost me my life. But I am willing to do what I have to. That's one thing I have always been good at."

He wasn't cozying up to me for a listening ear. "What do you want me to do?"

"I want you to prove that Chaska was behind the murder of that girl. I believe he has people spying for him and she was one of them. But I need proof to be able to have him tried before the council."

I eyed him. "And what do you get out of it?"

"I will become the acting chief."

So he was still trying to take the council. I wondered if this was all a ploy or if he really wanted to see change. I thought about it and shot him a counteroffer. "Make Yona chief and let Timothy come with me and you have a deal."

He frowned. "You drive a hard bargain, Miss Steele."

"I always do."

CHAPTER 35

THE DRIVE HOME WAS like a dream. Unreal, as if I watched my body from afar.

Joshua and Timothy talked in hushed voices in the front. Joshua came to get us as soon as I'd called him and gave him an update.

Hotah was a monster, and I knew that the only way to stop a monster is with a bigger monster. Something in me liked the thought, liked whatever I was gearing myself up for—what I might become.

I stared out the window as the black sky speckled with stars. It looked empty out there. All that remained were my thoughts. Thoughts of Yona and her burden. She begged me and Timothy to stop Hotah and Chaska. She said this would happen to more women if we couldn't get someone better as chief.

"Without a new chief, someone who cares about how women are treated and are not controlled by money, the tribe will be torn apart."

"Why don't you do something yourself, Yona? You're not helpless." I was angry at her for expecting me to do something when these were her people, her family. "You started the shelter, and the leader of the council is in love with you. If anyone has the power to change minds, it's you."

Yona hung her head. "I know, but I'm caught. If I keep quiet, I have money coming in, and I can use it to help. If I get cut off, it all goes down. No more shelter, no help for the girls. I can't risk it. That's why we need outside help."

Yona wasn't telling me everything she knew. I could see that she was hiding something, and her guilt was not just about this. But what else could there be?

Once we were on the road, Timothy looked at me in the rearview mirror. "Sarah, you've got to let this go. The best thing you can do is run. Keep away, and forget that I ever contacted you. When I reached out to you, I had no idea what it would mean. I can't have your life and your friends' lives on my hands."

"What about you? What about Yona?"

Timothy shrugged. "I'll do what I can, but for now I have to keep my distance. I'll publish my story and see if I can raise some awareness. And hope some other news sources pick it up and it creates a buzz. Yona will never leave the reservation. I was a fool to think she ever would."

My heart broke for him. He found love only to have it torn from him by the very one he loved. She had to stay in order to protect her family and by staying, she would lose the man she loved. Why did it have to be so hard?

CHAPTER 36

BY THE TIME I got home, it was after four in the morning. Timothy was sleeping on Joshua's couch, and I was so tired that I had trouble inserting the key into my apartment's deadbolt.

"Come on, little key, get in there."

I realized that it was already unlocked, and before my mental warning lights could flash, the door opened and Solomon pulled me into his arms. My body flexed and it took a full minute before I melted into him. Something about his warmth made me feel completely relaxed.

Tears welled up and I let them fall. Without a word, he scooped me up in his arms and carried me inside. I wanted to be strong, not to let him see me like this, but I was just too tired to care.

"Baby," he whispered. It wasn't a question, just a soft note of affection.

Placing me on the bed, he pulled off my shoes and socks and started taking my pants off. I let him. After I was tucked in, he slid in next to me and held me. I fell into a fitful sleep. For now, nothing mattered. I was in the arms of the one person I felt safe with. I was home.

CHAPTER 37

"GOOD MORNING, HOTTIE."

I opened one eye and groaned. Solomon stood beside my bed, holding a mug, and it smelled of coffee—glorious coffee.

"Go away. I want to be dead a little longer." I pulled the covers over my head and Solomon laughed. Not even coffee sounded better than the covers and more sleep.

"Come on, sleepyhead. It's getting late and if you stay in bed any longer, you'll miss my coffee-breath good-bye kiss."

I cursed. "And you might miss my zombie morning look."

"You do look a little undead. It's the hair."

I threw a pillow at him and he caught it. Sitting down on the edge of the bed, he looked at me and brushed my cheek with the back of his hand. I couldn't help but melt. "You are so beautiful." He kissed me and said, "For a zombie."

"Whatever. You were lucky I let you spoon me all night. My other boyfriends had to date me for a few years before they were allowed past the gates."

"I see. Well, I thank you, my lady. It was a great way to fall asleep.

Now, tell me about your adventure."

For the next hour, I told him everything that happened. Hotah killing two girls, the finger he threw at me, and my deal with Watters. Solomon listened and nodded in the right places, and as I was talking, something dawned on me, and I about kicked my own butt.

"What is it?" Solomon said.

I shook my head. I must have zoned out. "Why did he kill her?"

Solomon looked confused. "Who?"

"The girl, Lina Sever. She was talking to Timothy, but that was in secret and she was a known spy for Chaska. And even if they knew, they wouldn't kill her for that. So why did they kill her? How did I miss this? I mean, it should have been the first question I asked myself."

"Maybe she was a double agent of some kind, working for Chaska and Watters. If the other side found out, they would take her out, from what you describe. It would make sense."

I nodded. "That has to be it. I've gotta call—"

Solomon held up his hand. "Hold on now. I really don't like the idea of you going on with all this."

My jaw clenched. "What?"

Solomon sighed. "I don't want you to work this case anymore. It's too dangerous."

CHAPTER 38

PUSHING SOLOMON, I STRUGGLED out of bed, but the sheets were twisted around my legs. I was seconds from losing it, and I really didn't want to have another fight when things were going so well with him. But he had to stop trying to protect me.

"Let me clue you in. You don't get to tell me what I can and can't do. You get to support me, help me, but not put me on the sidelines just because you think I might get hurt."

Solomon stood up and glared down at me. I was still caught in my blasted web of a bed. "Hurt? Hurt? No, Sarah, this is more than that. You could get killed. Girls have died, and their murderers get away with it. What part of this don't you get? You're not a cop. This is not your job—"

Wrong. It is my job. I was hired to help Timothy—"

"And he told you to run. Your own client told you to go, to drop it so you would be safe. What more do you need?"

"I was just fine before you, and I don't need you to save me." I saw at once the hurt in Solomon's eyes. Why did I always do this—push away the people who loved me, build myself a wall and defend?

I rushed to tell him that I didn't need him, but that I wanted him. He stormed away before I could get the words out. What's wrong with me?

Swearing, I ripped the sheets off my legs and pulled on gym shorts and a tank top. I needed to work out, to blow off some stress and clear my head. My life felt like it was out of control, and I had to keep it from falling apart. If I melted, what would I turn in to then?

CHAPTER 39

SWEAT RAN DOWN MY back and soaked my tank top. I pounded the heavy bag with a knee, front kick, and knee combo. I wanted to vomit. I wanted to forget the world and lose my mind in a flurry of fists and feet.

Ducking as if an attacker was in front of me, I came up with my elbow and hit the bag hard. It was like seeing Hank Williams all over again, fighting for my life. It was like battling the Blondes—my body sucking air, trying not to drown or get shot in the face.

Jab, jab, hook.

I was crying and grinding my teeth as I punished the bag—and myself.

Leaning over, I wretched and threw up in the trashcan in the corner. I was so glad I was the only one in the fitness room because I was a mess, not fit for human viewing.

I felt better after my gut was empty, but I knew there was more in me—more anger and pain. Like something was knotted. How could I ever feel normal?

Solomon. My boyfriend, the man I was falling for—he just had to be the hero. Why did my prince have to be so freakin' . . . princey? I was not his little girl. Just let me take care of myself. I wanted a lover, not a father. I'd had enough of fathers.

I smashed the bag and let it all out.

Screw you, Hotah, you gutless sack of worthless flesh. Why won't you face someone your own size? And Yona, you hide like a mouse. You have the power to change things, but instead, you let murder and destruction continue on as you watch. How many more have to die, how many more have to get raped? I wanted to scream at Hotah, at Yona and the lot of them, get them all to wake up, but it wasn't my job. I got Timothy out. That was my job, and it was done. What more could I do?

Roundhouse, jab, jab, jab.

Now who was the lying rat? I stopped hitting the bag and sank to my knees. It wasn't Hank, Glenn, or even my parents—I was angry at myself. I was the one hiding in plain sight, keeping people away, and all these things in my life were just a reflection of what I was. I was hiding from myself.

I fought monsters because somewhere in me was one. I hated to see people hurt the ones around them because that's what I did. By keeping everyone out, I was hurting them. Even my best friend, Mandy, didn't know the real me. Did anyone know me?

It was time to stop running, stop hiding, and be who I was born to be. Whatever that was, I didn't know, but I knew I had to find out. If I had to be melted down and reformed into something new, so be it. I was ready.

CHAPTER 40

I CALLED JOSH AS I drove home from the gym.

"Hey, boss." His voice was a breath of fresh air.

"Hey, partner. Enough of this boss stuff."

"I like to annoy you, boss."

"I can see that. I need a favor."

Josh sighed. "I have a feeling that I am not going to like this favor. I thought we were done with this one."

"We are. Just trying to put a few things together for myself. Call it closure."

"Whatever you want, boss."

"I'm not sure what I want yet. Depends on if we get another case and more money. Oh, Timothy paid us. I saw that it went through this morning. We should have a company meeting and see how we want to spend this money. I vote Skittles. A lifetime supply of Skittles for each of us."

"Perhaps we should hire a CPA before you touch the money." He laughed. "Name the time and place and I'll be there. Now, what do you need?"

"I want you to find out who invested in the casinos back when they first started. Just see what you can dig up."

"Will do. What are you thinking?"

"Oh, that some of the investors may be connected to organized crime. Wouldn't they hate to have a press release stating that they're involved with a casino's crime ring? E-mail me the info when you're done."

I hung up and cursed the red light as I wound through downtown. I hit all green when I wasn't in a hurry, but today, all reds. It was time to take care of Hotah. I needed a record of him confessing to show to Watters. But more than that—he needed justice for what he'd done. I wasn't about to let him get away this easily. For a second, I was tempted to take him out to the desert and try every means of making him talk that I'd ever fantasized about. But even as the thought ran through my head, I knew that wasn't me—and it would change me in a way I could never recover from.

He needed justice—public justice. I not only wanted to out him in front of the law, but to shame him on his own turf. An idea flickered in my mind, and I smiled. If it worked, Hotah would be paid back in a very public way.

But first, I needed to do some research on him. I made it home and felt like I needed to go back to the gym after the stressful drive. Logging on to Google, I began my own version of research. I wouldn't dive into this unprepared.

After pulling up all Hotah's public records, I discovered that his dad had abandoned him when he was little, and his mother had been convicted of prostitution six times. She'd died from a drug overdose when Hotah was twelve, and he'd gone to live with his grandparents. His grandfather was a wife beater. She'd died under suspicious causes, but no one had ever been convicted. It was a trend in that county, it seemed. Then he'd gone in and out of friends' homes until he turned eighteen. He started working at the show when he was fourteen, and had received international acclaim for his archery skills. He bought a little cabin when he turned eighteen and an apartment when he was twenty. I was shocked to find out that he was only twenty-four. How had things gone so wrong for him? He had a tough life and I felt for him, but that was no excuse—he was a murderer.

I packed a backpack. I pulled my hair back in a cap, put gloves in my pocket, and laced on hiking boots. Then I opened my safe and packed my gun in my holster, which fit in the small of my back. I didn't intend to use it, but lots of things in life happen that you don't plan on. It was time for me to go hunting.

I called Mika. She sounded surprised to hear from me. "Figured you'd be long gone by now," she said.

"You can't get rid of me that easy. Has Hotah come into the casino yet today?"

"No, I haven't seen him, and from what I hear, he's banned from talking to me and Skah."

I told her part of my plan, and she gave me a few numbers for local doctors. She said she'd have the women's clinic open for me just in case. Perfect.

"Now all I have to do is get you a patient."

"Good luck!"

After that, I texted Mandy and Solomon, and my weekend of rest was underway. Don't bother me. I'm going to stay in bed and watch dumb action flicks and eat ice cream.

Getting in my car, I picked up a few items from the outdoor gear store. The usual—Coleman's oil, black powder, fire extinguisher, and zip ties. I grabbed a bag of Skittles, too. A good deed deserves its reward.

It felt so good to finally be free of the constraints I'd put on myself—I was thinking without walls, without rules. I couldn't stop grinning. "I'm coming for you, Hotah. This is your last show and there is going to be a surprise ending."

CHAPTER 41

HE WATCHED HER PULL out of her apartment parking garage and followed at a safe distance. She was prettier than he was told, but that meant nothing, really. Picking up his cell, he punched in a number and hit send.

After three rings, a woman answered. "What is it?"

The man spoke slow, deliberate. "I have her. She's going back."

"You have your orders. Follow her and take care of it."

"Done."

The man hit end and terminated the call. He had been bored the last few days and he was glad to get some action—or at least a distraction. There was nothing like a little chase to get the blood flowing.

He was a careful man, detailed, and he prided himself on being the best. It was not always easy being the best, but there were a few ways to ensure that his competition remained a distant second.

Training. He spent hours upon countless hours at the gun range, pushing his mind and body in the gym and sparring with the local MMA guys. He was fit, quick, intelligent, and deadly. But sometimes, pure psychical and mental conditioning was not enough. He ran across some who were bound to be a thorn in his side, so he hunted them and made sure they took an early retirement so he could remain at the top of the food chain.

So far he was the highest paid and most sought-after hit man in the lower 48. But he had plans to travel … maybe Dubai, or Shanghai.

Stepping from his car, he left the door open to draw the eye of anyone who might walk by and smoothly walked to Sarah's car. Dropping to a knee, he placed the tracking device under the right end of the fender. It was amazing how few people checked their cars for such devices or ever even thought to walk to the passenger side of their vehicle to inspect it before driving. He never failed to do so. He was no fool, and he banked on others being just that.

Standing, he turned and got back into his car and drove out of the parking garage. A sense of power washed over him, a knowing that he was not only in control, but he was the master of life and death.

Turning up toward Capital Boulevard, he made his way into the alley, parking in what the locals called "Freak Alley". Paintings, art, and other such nonsense cluttered the walls of the buildings in what to him looked like graffiti. One man's art was another man's defacement of public property.

Pulling up his GPS app, he saw that her car was still in the garage. Closing out the app, he opened another one—one he had made for him special—and it opened a live camera feed. She was in her living room on her laptop. He licked his lips and allowed himself a moment of preemptive pleasure.

Time to die, Sarah Steele.

CHAPTER 42

"A LITTLE BIRD TOLD me that you let Hotah bite you." Watters
sucked in on a cigar and blew smoke into Chaska's face.

"He is your creation, not mine." Chaska held his bandaged hand
and grimaced.

"I had nothing to do with him. Everyone knows he's insane and
I'm wondering how he got so close to you. Are you lost in his ways of
seduction or something?" He said it with a mocking air.

Chaska growled something unintelligible.

"Fix it," Watters said.

Chaska cursed. "What am I supposed to do?"

Watters glared at him, and his eyes betrayed a hunger for blood
that Chaska could feel in his bones. For a moment, he feared that
Watters was going to kill him right then and there, but instead, Watters
said, "Kill him—make him disappear. I don't care. Just take care of it."

Chaska turned in his chair, trying to break the tension in the room.
No wonder things were a total disaster. Like his favorite comic strip
Dilbert, he was surrounded by morons. He stood and poured himself
a glass of Cardhu 12 year and threw himself into his overstuffed chair

and closed his eyes.

Watters set his glass down and left without a word. Chaska could feel the stress crawl up his spine and wrap around his neck. He was caught in a web of his own making, and it was falling apart.

"Chaska…" The soft voice jarred him and his eyes shot open. Yona stood in the doorway with her hands folded in front of her. She peered up at him, and he felt his heart tighten.

"Yona. What brings you here?"

"We need to talk."

He hated when women said things like that. It was never a good thing—why couldn't they "need to talk" when it was good?

"Sit." He motioned to the plush chair in the corner. "Can I get you anything?"

Yona shook her head.

"What are you going to do about Hotah? He's killed three girls now, maybe more, and you almost hung an innocent man for something he didn't do."

Chaska gritted his teeth and held in his growing anger. "Your love, the reporter? There is no proof that Hotah had anything to do with that girl's death. As to the other thing—well, it is being taken care of."

Yona's face turned red. "Taken care of? That means it's being swept under the rug, It means you're going to keep pretending that everything's okay when it's clearly not."

"Yona, you overstep."

"No." There was a brightness to her eyes that he hadn't seen in years. "What happened to the man I once loved? The man of honor, the Chaska who was a proud chief of a proud people? Look at you. You're a cover-up man for a gang of thugs. This is nothing more than a mob."

"Enough." Chaska stood up and pointed to the door. "It's time for you to go."

Yona left and slammed the door so hard that the glass window in the top half shattered. Chaska raked his hand across his desk, sending the contents across the room.

Fumbling for his cell phone, he found Hotah's number and hit send. When the crazy kid answered, Chaska growled out his orders.

Hotah laughed. "It must be Christmas, because this is like ripping open the best present ever."

Chaska hated Hotah more than anyone he had ever met, but he was done playing games. "Just do it. Make it look like an accident."

"Will do, boss. I'll finish her after my next show."

CHAPTER 43

ONCE AT THE GOLDEN NUGGET, I pulled around to the delivery entrance, where food trucks were busy unloading. It was an overcast day, with the smell of a storm in the air. My hair stood on end and I took a deep breath. Time to start the chase.

Weaving through men carrying boxes and hauling dollies, I made my way to Hotah's dressing room with my bag of supplies. He wasn't there. The place was cluttered with cigarette butts and beer cans and trashy magazines. What a fine specimen of humanity he was. I took his costume from the rack and rushed down to the laundry room. After making my adjustments to the pants, I ran back up to his room and returned them to the rack. Then I leaned back in his chair, propped my feet on his makeup table, and closed my eyes. I relaxed entirely, putting everything from my mind.

The door opened behind me, but I didn't move. I could smell him, though. Day-old sweat and booze. He was finally here, and it gave me a thrill. There was not one doubt in my mind that he deserved what was coming to him. I pressed record on my phone.

Without turning, I said, "Time to confess to the murders, Hotah."

He grabbed the chair I was sitting in and swiveled it around, getting up in my face. His horrible breath made me lightheaded. "You don't want to mess with me—not right now and not in my own dressing room."

I gave him a pert smile. "I don't mess with people. I finish them."

His green eyes were creepy—they were wide and intense, like a snake zeroed in on its prey. "I'd like nothing more than to teach you some respect. But I've got orders."

"From who? The president?" I laughed.

He grunted. "I don't take orders from him."

"Who's your daddy, then?" I said in a baby's voice. I was trying to push every button he had. It was more fun for me than it should be, but I couldn't help it. I lived for this.

"You think I'm stupid?" he shouted.

I stood up and pushed him back. "You don't want me to answer that."

He raised his fist and my heart sped up. His reflexes were so slow, I knew I could dodge anything he threw my way and still stay three moves ahead. But he hesitated.

"Get out. I'm not going to talk to you. If you have a problem with me, talk to someone else."

I got an inch away from his face, gritting my teeth. He backed up half a step. "You killed those girls."

"No, I didn't." His eyes flitted back and forth. He was lying.

I wouldn't look away. He shifted his feet under my gaze, angry. "You know what happens to liars?" I said in a low voice.

He sneered at me. "What?"

"They burn," I whispered.

CHAPTER 44

THE SHOW STARTED IN ITS spectacular array of fireworks,
lights, and galloping horses, as usual. The crowd cheered and
clapped, "ooo"ing and "ahh"ing at the theatrics. I stood in the
shadows behind the entrance where the wagons rumbled out in
single file. Mika stood behind me. Her eyes were scared, but
determined. I gripped her hand and squeezed, willing her to be
strong and stay beside me.

"Here it comes," I said. "If only it'll work."

Hotah galloped out on a gorgeous black horse, shirtless and proud.
The bonfire in the middle of the arena flickered and snapped. Smoke
trailed up to the ceiling. His arrow was padded with an oil-soaked tip
for his fire trick. He gave a war cry that sent shivers down my spine.
He reached the middle of the stage and backflipped off the horse as he
pulled back the bow. Almost time. Little Annie ran into the arena just as
fake pigeons dropped from the ceiling. She shot them all down as the
crowd cheered.

Hotah's turn. "Aiaiaiaiai," he cried, and then stuck his arrow in the
fire.

"Come on," I whispered. All it needed was a spark.

He shot an arrow at a target and it burst into flame.

"No!" It didn't work. All of this had been for nothing. "Time for plan B," I said to Mika.

"Wait," she said, staring at Hotah.

The crowd whooped and hollered again. Hotah raised his arms in the air, took a step back, and bowed. A spark from the bonfire jumped out and landed on his pants. They burst into flames with a loud whoosh. He screamed like a girl. White-and-yellow flames consumed his legs and smoke covered his body. He sprinted for the exit—our exit—his eyes panicked. As he passed, I grabbed his arm and threw him against the wall. He hunched his shoulders, gasping. Raising the fire extinguisher, I sprayed it at the flames. People surrounded us. Mika barked at them to give us space. White powder filled the hallway.

Hotah slumped to the ground. The flames had burned bright and hot, but not for long. I doubted the burns were deep, but they'd be painful. He trembled and moaned, his eyes clenched shut.

"Should we call an ambulance?" a girl said in a panicked voice.

"No," I said, hauling him up. He cried out, and I can't say I even felt a twinge of compassion.

"We're taking him to the hospital now," Mika said.

"Or thereabouts," I whispered.

CHAPTER 45

HE WAS A CRYING, drooling mess on the exam bed. The lighting was low. His pants were charred and red, and swollen skin was exposed. He trembled violently and then screamed, "Get me a doctor!"

I grabbed his wrists and tied both his hands to the bed's rail. "What are you doing?" he yelled.

A female doctor and nurse walked in, crossing their arms across their chests. Their faces were like stone. Mika glared at him from the corner.

I pointed my finger in his face. "How does it feel?"

He writhed in agony and screamed at us again like a wild animal.

"Now you know what it's like to be alone, in pain, with no hope of anyone standing up for you. This is what the girls you attacked went through."

"Argh! Get me to the hospital!" He pulled his hands, but the restraints held fast.

I leaned in and he bit at me, so I jerked my head back. "Whoa there. You know your boss just ratted you out? The police will be here to arrest you any minute." I silently pressed record on my phone again.

He ground his teeth and tried to wrench his hand out of the zip tie. "Chaska owes me! He's mine! There's nothing but cowards' blood in him. He's soft and afraid. I'm the true leader of the tribe." He growled. "I don't do anything for him that I don't want to do." Aha, there it was. He was singing like a canary. His eyes rolled back in his head and he gasped from the pain. "And those girls," he whispered. "I was doing them a favor. They were traitors to the tribe. I set them free."

I leaned forward and whispered in his ear. "Do you want to be set free, Hotah?"

He hauled back and tried to headbutt me. I easily dodged. "Get away from me! Get away! I will get you back for this!" He motioned to Mika. "I will see you all dead."

"A fool digs his own grave, Hotah."

We left him to his screaming. It was a pathetic end for a pathetic man. I had what I needed for Watters—this confession would solidify his place as the new chief, and than he could elect Yona as leader and turn Chaska in to the authorities.

Mika was crying, tears pouring down her cheeks.

"What is it?" I put a hand on her shoulder.

"I just can't believe our chief is the one who ordered the murder. He must have known Lina was talking with Timothy." Her bottom lip trembled. "I hate the thought of him working against his own people that way. It's all so horrible. If it weren't for you coming here—I can't believe it worked."

I gave her a hug. "It's time for you to get a good leader. Now wipe up your tears. We've got a lot of work to do."

I texted Yona that an emergency elders' meeting needed to be called—and everyone had to be there.

Mika wiped the tears from her eyes.

I looked up at her, and something suddenly dawned on me. "It was you."

From her expression, I judged she knew exactly what I was talking about. "And Skah," she said.

The pieces finally fell in the puzzle. "You found Lina and knew Hotah had been hired, and knew he'd never be prosecuted. So you dragged her body into Timothy's car."

Guilt and sadness flashed over her face. "It was awful, finding her. And the last straw. That's when I knew we had to get someone from the outside involved. I'm so glad it was you."

I smiled. "Well, it's not over yet."

"I'm ready to stop working for that stupid show." She smiled. "And start working on my next novel."

"Let's settle this once and for all so you can get on with your life." I squared my shoulders and strode outside, feeling like things might work out after all.

CHAPTER 46

"THE COUNCIL IS CALLED to order," Chaska said after the drums stilled. He held up a wounded hand and I put two and two together. Hotah took his finger and would have taken the tribe as well if it wasn't for Watters.

"Yona has called this emergency meeting in order to deal with—"

Watters stood and interrupted. "I would like to take the floor, if you don't mind, Tate." Chaska flushed red in the cheeks, but nodded.

"Thank you." I knew what was going to happen. Watters would accuse Chaska of murder, of hiring Hotah to kill for him. He would call for Chaska's immediate removal as chief and to vote Yona in as acting chief. We went over the details in person before the show and I had his word. I felt like this was the last play before things were set right.

We sat in a circle in the old room. Dust filtered through the light beams that shone on the floor. The tension was thick. Everyone was eyeing each other as if they were about to be stabbed in the back. Yona looked stronger than I'd ever seen her—she held her chin high, she'd worn a long skirt, and there was a fierce light in her eyes. She looked like a queen. Chaska looked scared and in pain, though he tried to hide it. He eyed me distastefully, as if I were garbage he couldn't wait to throw out. Watters was as calm and businesslike as usual.

"I have been doing a lot of thinking, and with the feud, bloodshed, and lawlessness going on around here unchecked, it has forced me to take action." Watters shot me a look and continued. "I was informed by Miss Steele that she has some evidence to share with the council, and I believe you all should hear her out." He paused. "Miss Steele?"

Tahatan stood in the doorway with a young man also in uniform.

I was only allowed in the council meeting because Watters got me past Tahatan. In this case, money talked, and Tahatan knew who signed his checks. I set my phone on the little table and pushed play. They heard Hotah hollering his confession. Mutters and whispers filtered through the council. Chaska cringed when he heard his name and then his face wrinkled in anger. "Stop this!" he said, fear flashing in his eyes.

Yona's face darkened. "Exactly. We need to stop this." She stood, and Watters lifted his hand to gain the floor.

"Based on this confession and the detailed report Miss Steele and her associates have provided me, I am placing you under arrest." Motioning to Tehatan, Watters still did not move to introduce Yona, but he was gearing up for something.

The council bubbled over, people talking over each other, Chaska yelling and waving his arms wildly. My alarm bells went off and I watched Yona, vowing to protect her if it got any more out of hand.

"Quiet!" Watters boomed. He held up a talking stick and the people calmed. Some even sat down again. "I hold the talking stick and I have the floor." Chaska put his hands on his hips and glared at Tehatan and Watters. No one moved, and Tehatan seemed confused as to what to do.

Yona pointed at Chaska. "I've defended you my whole life, hoping that one day you'd remember who you were and see what you've become. I used to love you!" Yona's voice cracked, but she recovered. "What you've done, been a part of… it makes me sick. I hope you rot in an American prison."

Chaska lunged at her. I rushed forward. Taking a defensive stance, I kicked his knee. With a cry, he went down. I punched him in the temple, and he didn't move. Two-hit knockout. My kick-boxing training had served me well.

"He's done here," I said.

Tahatan came forward, a heavy crease to his brow. "You sure you want to start this, lady? That's our chief!"

"Not anymore," Watters said, holding up a hand. "I am stepping in as acting chief, as head of the family and rightful bloodline of the tribe." No one moved and my face was throbbing. He was going to betray us—his own tribe and his sister. "I had the votes anyway, and now that Chaska's crimes have come to light, this is the way it must be."

Yona went pale. She moved her mouth, but no words came out. Watters turned to Tahatan. "I told you to arrest him. Now do your job or I'll have you removed from your position and have someone put in who can follow orders."

Tahatan slid his hand to his sidearm, then pointed a finger at me. "You ruined everything! I'm not going to let you get away with this." Glaring at Watters, he cursed and spun around, storming out muttering.

I relaxed when I heard his truck rumble away. I could see that Watters and our evidence had won the council--they looked to Chaska with hatred. I cursed myself for trusting Watters, and now he had the council and the casinos, just like he always wanted. Yona was shifting her weight and I knew that her anger would eventually turn to submission if something didn't happen, and soon.

Watters spoke up. "Because of this betrayal of our people, we risk our laws being overruled by the laws of the U.S. government. We risk losing our right to be a tribe, our way of life."

Watters turned to the remaining tribal police and commanded

them to arrest Chaska. "Put Chaska in the holding cell and then I'll file proper charges against him."

Two men in uniform stepped forward and took Chaska. They cuffed his hands behind his back and held his arms, and Yona faced Watters. "You made a deal. You promised. How could you?"

He hesitated. For a moment, he looked so old and sad. "You never did understand how the real world works." Lifting his hand, he said loud enough for all the council to hear, "Yona will be the new head of the tribal police and oversee that justice is done, that the abuse against women comes to an end!" With this, the council cheered, and I wanted to tear his head off. He lied, and now he was making himself look like a hero.

Yona took his hand, and with more self-control than I've ever seen, she said, "Greed. Power. They turn people into something unrecognizable. Old ideals are smothered by a lust for more."

She was going to make a great leader—she could stop the crime at the casinos and keep everyone safe. What started out as simply getting Timothy free from a false murder charge had led to a change in the whole system, yet it all left a bitter taste in my mouth. Watters used me, and I would not rest until I found out to what extent he was involved and if the casinos were still going to be in the underground smuggling operation.

Yona came up to me with a look of sullen victory in her eyes. "Well, I guess things didn't go as we planned. I'm so angry with my brother for using this situation for his personal gain. I should've known better."

"We both should have seen it coming, but I wanted to believe him. So, what now?"

Yona sighed. "I do what I can with the power I have. The girls will be safe and I'll do what I can to make sure my brother stays on the right path. He may have won this battle, but I plan to win the war."

I hugged Yona tight, and tears welled up in my eyes. "You are going to make a great chief one day. This is your tribe, you are a great leader, and most of all—you care. I am so proud of you."

"I owe it all to you, Sarah. You believed in me, and that made me want to stop hiding. Thanks for putting yourself on the line for me, for us."

I hoped that Yona would have what it took to keep in front of her brother, but a part of me wondered if she could. He was not only smart, but he was ruthless. Yona was nothing close to ruthless, and sometimes bad things have to happen to make things change for the better.

Yona was talking to a group of council members and Watters was grilling Chaska. They were in some sort of deep, heated conversation and I half listened, suddenly wanting to be home. The longing for Solomon's arms around me was acute. Then my cell buzzed in my pocket "Hello?"

"It's Mika. Hotah escaped. He got free somehow and knocked out the doctor, and the nurses were locked in a closet!"

I cursed fiercely, striding to the exit. I knew exactly where he was heading.

"Sarah, what are we going to do? He's dangerous."

I closed the phone and walked into the night. "So am I."

CHAPTER 47

I COULD SEE LIGHT up ahead, so I killed the headlights and stopped my car. I wanted to go in on foot, keep the element of surprise for whatever I planned to do. I didn't have much more of a plan than that. Most of it was to get in unseen and take Hotah in whether he liked it or not.

I glanced up at the stars and glowing moon and felt a wave of peace fill me. This was who I was. This was what I was supposed to do. Hunt the bad guys down and give them what they gave out.

Taking my car keys, I put them in my pocket and double-checked my gun. It felt good having it there. If he was in there, for sure, his truck sat parked out front.

I unzipped my backpack and took out the package of zip ties and duct tape. I put a few ties in my pocket and made sure I had a spare set of clothes just in case. I closed the trunk as quietly as I could and began walking toward the light blazing on the porch of the cabin. The cabin was old and rotting—what an eyesore. A rusted-out truck sat on the lawn, and junk littered the porch. There was one door and two small windows in the front of the cabin—this would be a good place to set up.

Crickets and cicadas and frogs made a cacophony of noise, muffling my steps. The woods surrounding the cabin were thick and choked with brush. The hair on my neck stood on end and I got the unmistakable feeling that someone was watching me.

The thought that I was taking this a little far did cross my mind, but like a good little crazy person, I stuffed it under. Maybe the skill of stuffing feelings could work for me instead of against me.

"Hold it right there." A low voice spoke behind me. "Ah, hands up and turn around slowly. You think you were alone?"

I turned. Tahatan held a handgun straight at my head. He must have parked somewhere else and walked back here to take care of Hotah.

"Tahatan, why on earth would you defend such a piece of pond scum like Hotah? Have you no pride?"

"What makes you think I was here to help him?" He swallowed. "Hotah's a loose end, and I hate loose ends."

I laughed. "So you plan on killing him?"

"What are you doing here, Miss Steele? I thought you got your way. You even managed to get out of jail and yet here you are again, shoving your nose where it doesn't belong."

"I thought I'd bring in reinforcements." I put my hands behind my back casually, feeling the familiar bulge of my gun. "You know—the FBI, the police, a few of my friends from the DA's office."

This time Tahatan laughed. "Nice try, but you are alone. I watched you drive in all by yourself."

"Okay, so now what?" I hadn't put a round in the chamber yet. Tahatan had his gun at his hip, held loose in his hands. Could I draw faster than him? The thought gave me a thrill. He hadn't even checked to see if I was armed. The best part about being a woman was that I was constantly underestimated.

"I think we should go for a walk." He motioned with his gun to the dark forest. "I don't want to have to drag a body if I can get you to walk to your grave before I kill you."

He was going to kill me. "You think ahead. Good for you."

I walked toward the tree line. The thick grass caught on my ankles, and I let it slow me down. If the distance between us was shortened, I'd have a better chance of beating him or catching him off guard. It was the longest walk I'd ever taken. My senses were on full alert—my skin tingled and my heart surged with adrenaline.

When I walked through the tree line and into a small open area, I saw that a hole had been half dug. A shovel stuck in the dirt like an arm pointing to the sky—or a grave marker. I expected a bullet anytime. My hands trembled, and I took a deep breath. The moon cast a glow on everything. I heard a rustle of clothing as he raised his arm. This was it.

I dove behind a tree and pulled out my gun as I landed. He shot and bark splintered, showering me with grit. I rolled and came to my feet on the other side of the tree, firing twice. Tahatan staggered back three steps and fell to his knees. The gun slipped from his fingers. He looked at me in shock. "You had a gun?"

I blew the smoke from my barrel. "The great Tahatan, beaten by a girl."

He gurgled blood and fell face forward in the dirt.

I held my position for a minute and when no one came running, I slid my gun back into its holster. I thanked Solomon silently for encouraging me to keep up my shooting. The gun range knew my name and I felt comfortable with it now, like it was a part of me.

My heartbeat pounded in my ears. I let out a long breath. There was so much energy in me, I felt as if I were on fire, as if I could do anything. Was this what true power felt like? I had finally accepted who I was, and it felt amazing.

Now I had to hide my tracks. Tahatan was a big man, and the hole was meant for me. I holstered my weapon and grabbed the shovel. It was soft dirt, so the digging was not that hard, but I was sweating buckets by the time I was done.

I rolled him to the grave. By the time I got him there, I was covered in dirt and my muscles trembled with fatigue. I pushed him in and he lodged at the bottom of the hole. I covered him, put a few big rocks on top, and moved some underbrush on top to mask the fresh dirt. After that, I covered my tracks around the site, rearranging the grass I'd plowed through, rustled up crushed leaves, and buried my footprints in the dirt. It wasn't a perfect cover-up, as any dog would be able to find him on a warm day, but it was good enough for me.

Thirty minutes ago, I was led into the forest to die, but now I came out the victor. Triumph surged through me as I walked to the brightly lit cabin with my shovel in hand. I figured I might need it again before the night was through.

CHAPTER 48

IT WAS NOT A brilliant plan, but it was something. I was hunting, running on pure instincts, and it felt good. Was it smart, immoral? I didn't care—it was what I felt I had to do. I had to make things right somehow, even if that meant killing along the way.

I did a circle around the cabin and saw Hotah sitting on a ragged couch in the living room with a bottle in his hand. He was alone. Maybe he would be drunk by now and kill himself with pain meds. I figured he would be in serious pain with how bad his burns were.

I held my gun out in front of me and down, like Solomon showed me back when I first learned gun safety, took a deep breath, and opened the door. It creaked on its hinges. I jumped in the room and dodged to the left in case Hotah was armed.

The couch was empty, and before I could react, I heard the unmistakable pop and electric crackle of a Taser. Something struck me in the shoulder. My body wrenched in pain and every muscle convulsed. I fell to the ground, shaking, my teeth chattering. Tears ran unbidden down my cheeks and I groaned.

My mind shut off and everything was a blur. Funny thing about pain—it makes everything else seem not to matter. I just wanted it to stop.

Hotah's fuzzy form limped from the corner. I gasped for breath, but I couldn't get my lungs to cooperate. My muscles didn't respond, but my mind was alert and overloading all at the same time—I was helpless. He leaned down and jammed something into my neck. It stung and then his hand trailed down my chest. Screams rose in my throat, but I couldn't get them out.

"Your skin is so smooth." He still smelled of charred flesh and his voice echoed like we were in a large bathroom. "It's not going to be so smooth after I cut you again and again."

Think, Sarah. Focus on one thing. Try to relax.

Hotah looked around and he came into view a little clearer now as the electricity began to fade away, but I felt weird, and unable to move like I should. "You meant to get me alone, didn't you? You have the hots for me. I could see it in your eyes the first time we met. You want me—you all do. It's not a stretch to believe that you white girls would want a little dark meat." He grinned, and there was something in his eyes that scared me. There was a monster in there—I knew well what it looked like. "You didn't have to burn me to get my attention, but maybe that's your thing. Are you into the hard stuff? Like it rough, huh?"

"Dirty . . . bastard," I choked out.

I had been so foolish to underestimate Hotah. My own pride and zest for the chase got in the way of my common sense. But it wasn't over yet. I thought fast, sizing up the room and looking for an out. The place was filthy. The floor was covered in dirt clumps and dust. A little bed, without a frame, sat in a corner with a ratty quilt on it. There was another room, but I couldn't tell if it was a bathroom or bedroom. A fireplace took up one wall and I spied a little shovel, broom, and poker that could be used as weapons. The shovel I had with me lay a few feet away—that was my best bet. I couldn't find my gun I must have dropped it when I got Tasered.

"I gave you something to calm your nerves, it is mild but should make you feel good, don't you want to feel good?" He chuckled. "I'm gonna prepare a little place for you over here so you'll be comfortable in the days to come." He limped to a chair and set it in front of the fireplace, then attached four handcuffs—one on each leg.

Hotah looked over his shoulder at me and winked. "You know this is where I killed my grandmother?" He laughed. "She didn't fight me, but then, she didn't really think I'd do it."

With all my might, I tried to move. I felt a bit of warmth in my fingers—was the feeling returning?

He leaned over me, pressing his cheek against mine. And he bit my ear. Oh, God. Please, God. Let my feeling return. "Your blood tastes good." He pulled the Taser darts out and scooped me up in his arms and moaned in agony when I my body brushed against his burned thighs. Heat swept up my body. This was it!

I swung my fist, connecting with his chin. Hotah's head snapped around. He dropped me. I rolled to my feet and lunged forward, but fell facefirst as my legs gave out. Crawling away from him, I managed to get my feet under me, and when I was up, he was on top of me. "You do like it rough. You'll pay for that one kitten!" He thought this was a game? He was insane, and his speech seemed a little off kilter but maybe that was due to whatever he injected me with.

I dodged his fist and hooked my ankle behind his and pushed him back. He fell, hard. He screamed a curse and writhed on the floor.

Scrambling for the shovel I spotted my gun under the edge of the couch. I reached out and grabbed the gun holding it with two hands. "Hands up, Hotah! Not a move, not a single move. My hands are all shaky from that Taser, so I may shoot you by accident."

Hotah was on his back and blood seeped from his lip. Our eyes met and he spat at me.

"You nasty whore." Hotah wriggled, trying to get to his feet, and I steadied the gun and pointed it at his face. He froze and raised his hands.

I pressed my hand against my ear to stem the bleeding. "Sit down in that chair." I motioned to the wooden chair he'd prepared for me.

"And if I don't?" He should have been scared, but he seemed more annoyed than anything else.

"If you don't, I'll kill you," I stated in a flat tone.

"You don't have the guts. You're just a girl." He was on his rear with his knees up and his hands in the air, but as he talked, he was lowering them.

I shot him in the kneecap. He yelped like a wounded dog and collapsed, clutching his bloody knee.

"Next one is to your head." My voice trembled. Not from fear or terror, but from pure rage. I was using every ounce of my self-control not to plug him in the face.

"You crazy bitch." Hotah dragged himself to the chair and pulled himself up into it, breathing hard. I smiled tightly.

Hotah sneered at me, both hands over his bloody leg. Blood seeped through his fingers. I could smell it, its rich, vibrant scent.

That switched something inside me. "You like killing women, don't you, Hotah."

He laughed. "They deserved it, but that's not all I like to do. Come closer ad I'll show you."

Walking behind him, I was still a little woozy but able to snap the cuffs into place around his hands first and then his ankles. He moaned through gritted teeth and muttered a curse.

"And Lina Sever—did she deserve it?"

"She got off easy. She was a rat. I should have killed that stupid reporter, too."

I wanted to keep him talking. The more he talked, the stronger I
felt. "You're just a lapdog to Chaska. You've never had an original idea
in your life."

Hotah rattled his restraints and cursed. "I'm no one's lapdog. You
think you have it all figured out, think you know what's going on here?
You know nothing. I tell you what I want you to know, and what are
you? You're nothing." If he was drunk or high on something, the shot
to his knee must have sobered him up.

I winked at him. "Wow, you really thought that would work? Let
me guess. In your little childlike mind, I would get angry because
you're insinuating that I'm weak. Maybe I'd even slip up and give you
a chance to get the upper hand? Come now, I thought you were smarter
than that."

Hotah grinned. "Yeah, I guess I did. So what now—you gonna
shoot me again?"

His face wrinkled and he licked his lips, scanning my body up
and down. "Now run away and go call your white cop buddies. Have
them get the Justice Department to come and slap me on the wrist." He
laughed. "This isn't your place—it's my place. Now get the hell out!"

He was right. I could send evidence to the Idaho State Police or
to Solomon and ask him to pass it to the right people. I would send it
to Timothy James and Yona—have them spread the news through the
country. Everything might wrap up in a neat little package, but it wasn't
enough. Lina Sever, his grandmother, the two casino girls, and however
countless other victims deserved more, and I couldn't deny it. I needed
more. I could feel the tension in my shoulders, the desire to give in to
the need growing in me.

"You're right, Hotah. The only way to end this is to end you."
My back was to him. I spun around and squeezed the trigger and put a
bullet into his forehead. Blood sprayed the fireplace behind him, and
his eyes rolled back in their sockets.

Something in me released and I found that I was breathing hard. My skin tingled. And as much as I hate to admit it, I felt alive. Hotah's head slumped backward and his body went limp. I should have been horrified, should be sickened by what I'd just done, but all I could feel was the surge of life that was flowing through me.

"Why?" I said to the air. But it was not, Why did I just kill a man who was tied up and who I could have easily sent to jail. It was, why did I want to kill him? Why did I like killing him?

That was the question my soul would have to answer. But not right now.

I felt myself reshaping into something new. Something stronger. Something truer. For the first time in my life, I knew that this was a part of me I could no longer ignore. I couldn't just hide the demons in the dark and pretend they weren't there. Time to face them and live up to who I was.

CHAPTER 49

I LEFT HOTAH EXACTLY where he was, but I searched the ground where I had been Tasered for any signs of hair or lint I may have dropped. It was so dark, I couldn't be sure. My DNA would be all over the cabin, so I grabbed the bottle of Vodka he was drinking and poured it all over him and around him on the floor. I removed the handcuffs and put them in the cabinet under the sink next to the scrub brushes. That should do it. They would find him shot and Tahatan missing and figured Tahatan shot him and left town. At least, that's what I hoped they'd believe.

I walked through the cabin one last time, put the shovel next to the door, and threw the Taser into the fireplace. I was about to leave when something stopped me. He was shot, and them believing that he was killed and the killer was missing was too far-fetched. It had to be an open-and-shut case.

After a moment, I came to the only conclusion I could, and it would be poetic to boot. Suicide. I walked back outside and dug through Hotah's truck. Come on, you have to have something I can use. I didn't want the gun to come back to me, and there had to be a gun. My idea was that he was in pain and guilty, so he drank himself silly and shot himself. The bullet sparked the spilled Vodka and the cabin went up in flames. It wasn't perfect, but it was darn good on short notice.

There.

Hotah had a small nail file on his key ring and they dangled in the ignition. It took some doing, but I managed to file the serial numbers off my weapon. I hoped that it would be burned enough to destroy any DNA. If not, I could say he stole it from me. I laughed in spite of myself for how dumb this all was. Yona was the new tribal police and this was a reservation. The chance of this even going to court or even getting back to me was slim.

Tossing the keys on the kitchen counter, I lit a rolled-up newspaper and watched Hotah ignite. Somehow it was beautiful and horrible all at the same time. Leaving the cabin, I got back into my car and drove away with flames rising in my rearview mirror.

CHAPTER 50

ALL I WANTED WAS a shower and to go to bed and forget the whole thing. But I was a complete mess and still had to make sure things with Yona were okay. I'd left in a hurry and no one knew where I was. Mika would be the only link to the truth, and I didn't think she would talk.

Every muscle in my body was still sore from the Taser, and my ear throbbed. The bleeding had stopped, but there was going to be a scar. I picked up my cell and called Mika back.

"Hey Mika, can I come over to your house? I need to talk to you."

"Sure. Are you okay?" She sounded concerned. "Yona was looking for you. We're are all down at the casino, but you can use my place if you want. I'll come let you in."

"Thanks, and don't tell anyone anything, okay?"

"Uh, okay, sure."

I hung up and drove to the address she texted me. Mika lived in a modest home that was still beautiful by today's standards. Her car was parked in the driveway, and I pulled in next to hers and got out.

"Sarah!" Mika bounded from the front of the house and stopped dead in her tracks when she saw me. "Whoa, you look awful!"

"I know. But you should see the other guy."

"Come inside. Let's get you cleaned up. You can wear some of my clothes if you want."

"It's okay—I have a fresh set in my trunk. Old habit from college days," I said.

The shower was glorious. And afterwards, I told Mika what happened, but left out the part about Tahatan and added in a few details such as Hotah attacked me, took my gun, and I shot him in self-defense. A fire broke out, and I ran and lost my gun. Every good lie was laced with truth, and this one was one I felt like I had to tell.

"So I need you to cover for me if my name ever comes up in connection to Hotah's death."

Mika hugged me and kissed my cheek. "You were never there, and all I told Yona was that he escaped. I'll make sure this never comes back on you, Sarah. You saved us. I owe you this."

"Thanks, Mika."

After my hair was dry, we both drove into town but in our own cars. I put my bloody clothes in a bag in the trunk to deal with later and felt a huge sense of release. I knew that I'd never be free from what I'd done, but I needed to sever as many connections as I could.

When I pulled into the valet parking drive of the Golden Nugget, Yona was there. She looked tense and worried—what was going on? Why was she out there, as if waiting for someone?

I jumped out of the car. "What is it, Yona?"

She set her jaw. "I'm glad you're here, Sarah. I need to set things right with Watters, and after everything that's happened, I can't go on being quiet about the truth."

Then the world erupted in a volley of sirens, flashing lights, and yelling. Men dressed in riot gear, SWAT trucks, and men with FBI printed on the backs of their jackets swarmed the building. I grabbed

Yona and we made for a corner to get out of the way.

"FBI. Everybody down. This is the FBI. Put your hands up." I could have picked Solomon out of any crowd and he led the charge with his Glock out, looking like a world-class stud.

People were screaming and running around. A helicopter beat the air overhead. The FBI and SWAT team had the area locked down in a matter of minutes.

Yona's face was full of satisfaction.

"You did the right thing," I told her. "They'll find all the drugs, guns, and girls in the basement and have this place cleared out."

"And closed down," she said. Then she took a deep breath. "We'll rise through other means."

I took her hand. "Nothing will keep you down."

Someone touched me on the shoulder. It was Timothy James and Solomon stood behind him, smiling at me.

"You really know how to party," Timothy said. He hugged me, and I was so glad to see him. "My editor says this is the best investigative article I've ever done. And I'm finishing up a huge personal interest article on Miss Yona Watters." He gave her a side hug and she glowed with happiness.

"Pulitzer Prize, here you come! Now, you two go find a quiet place somewhere."

Yona winked at me and they walked off, hand in hand.

Solomon stood a few feet away with his hands at his sides. The chaos behind him made it seem like he was frozen in time. I walked to him, swinging my hips from side to side like I used to do when I was in high school.

"Hi," I said.

"Hi."

He looked so good. I wanted to be angry with him, but I just couldn't. "You have to stop barging in on me. It's totally indecent."

"But what if I like barging in on you?"

"Hmm, I guess we could work something out. You got a white horse to take me away on?"

Solomon took both my hands and pulled me in close. "No, you're more of a black dragon sort of girl. Now kiss me."

I decided that this command I would obey, but only because I wanted to. Lucky him.

CHAPTER 51

SOLOMON HAD TO DO a ton of paperwork, but he was going to come over after he was done. I had promised him a backrub and a bottle of wine. I loved being with him, even if he frustrated me at times.

I was almost to Boise, driving my trusty car back home. Mandy made me swear to go to coffee in the morning with her and Joshua so we could plot our new company and go over everything that had happened in the last few days. I agreed.

A white BMW was following me—at first I thought we were just part of the traffic heading from the casino to Boise, but when I pulled off at the exit, the BMW took the exit too. My alarm bells went off and I mentally ran through my options.

After gassing up at a truck stop, I checked my voicemail and texts. My poor phone was flooded with texts from both Mandy and Solomon. They went from inquiring to annoyed to worried.

One from Joshua simply said Call me.

It wasn't too late and I was still a good thirty minutes out, so I dialed him. After two rings, he answered.

"Do I get extra pay for working after hours?" he asked.

"Ha, no way. I've been on the job for days."

"Slave driver."

"Yeah, yeah. So, what do you have for me? Tell me some good news."

Joshua sighed. "Not sure it's good news, but it is news. I did a search on the casinos, like you asked. Some of the first investors were hard to track down, but once I found out their real names, I got a good line on where to go from there."

"And what did you find out?"

"Seems your best buddy at Williams, Inc. had a vested interest in the groundbreaking."

My brain kicked into overdrive and I looked in the rearview mirror to make sure the BMW with the mystery man was still there. It was.

"You sure?"

"Yup, I'll e-mail you all my research. But something else, Sarah. This thing is much bigger than I think you know. The underground smuggling system is not just this tribe, not just one reservation."

"I know. Something like this has to be bigger."

"Yeah, try nationwide, as in, 90% of them are all linked back to Williams, Inc. Think about it. They're not under U.S. law, they run by their own rules—it's the perfect pipeline for smuggling. Even if they get caught, no one can do anything about it."

"What do you mean? How can that be? Why would they—" But why not? Like the mob back in old Chicago, organized crime was like any business. It needed outlets, a way to get goods in and out. If Williams, Inc. was involved, than it was just as I suspected—they weren't just developing energy-efficient batteries, paving the way to taking over energy development. That was their offense. They were playing defense as well, taking over as the new mob, except no one knew it.

"I see by your silence that you're putting the pieces together," Joshua said.

I nodded. "Yeah, this is big, Josh. I mean, really big. Like, we could spend our whole lives on it big."

"Or die for it big. These guys are ruthless. I think we may need some help on this one, Sarah. If this is just one arm of their operation and Rio was another, who knows what else they control. They're dangerous, and you're on their radar."

I hated to admit it, but he was right. I had the tiger by its tail and it was turning to bite me. I glanced into the rearview mirror once more and muttered to myself.

"Who are you, and what do you want?"

CHAPTER 52

I WAS AT MY favorite local coffee joint, at my favorite side table with the cushy chairs, drinking my favorite drink. Life had finally returned back to normal.

"Chai tea? What happened to your coconut coffee?" Mandy had on a leather jacket, boots with spikes, and her hair up and tangled around a No. 2 pencil.

"I'm trying to kick the coffee and go with tea instead."

"Why? Coffee rocks." Mandy sipped her mocha, and Joshua wisely stayed out of the conversation.

"And your outfit this morning rocks as well." I rolled my eyes.

"You're just jealous."

"Extremely."

Joshua munched on a bran muffin and had a stack of paperwork in front of him.

"Okay, Joshua, what do you have for us?"

"Oh, just some contracts. It makes our little adventure all legal and real, so to speak."

Mandy groaned. "Boring—so we become an LLC or S Corp. Who

cares. Tell me what's going to happen to Yona and that creepy guy."

"Well, according to Solomon, Watters and Chaska were arrested. Both will serve jail time, probably life sentences. Hotah's body, or what remained of it, was found in a little cabin. It seems that there was a fire. They're not sure what happened, but it could be a suicide. Tahatan, their chief of police, is missing, but it looks like the FBI is going to let the tribal police do most the heavy lifting. Yona has a mess to weed through—I'm glad I'm not in her shoes. But she's completely capable. All the drugs, weapons, and such were confiscated, and that little stop on the pipeline is out of commission."

"Cool—we so rock. I mean, we did that. Well, you did most of it, Sarah."

I snorted. "So glad you noticed."

Sipping my tea, I scanned the road over Joshua's shoulder and saw the same white BMW that had been following me for the last few days parked up the block.

Joshua cleared his throat. "We got lucky. In the future, we need to have a plan. I want clear communication, not this run–and-gun sort of thing." He eyed me as if I was the culprit.

I turned to stare at Joshua. "But I like guns."

He frowned. I held up my hand. "No, I'm sorry. You're right—I should have been better at communicating. Next time I'll do better." He smiled and shook his head.

As they talked about where to get an office and what kind of logo we should have, I tried to concentrate, but like a magnet to metal, I was pulled toward the BMW. We needed to have a proper introduction. My mind spun with ideas on the best way to provide that opportunity. It was all so natural and easy—this ability to hunt and catch, seek and find. No longer did I feel any need to push it down or quiet it. This was me. And I felt free.

I would seek justice for the innocent. With or without the law behind me.

SWEET DREAMS

Book 1 in the WJA series
A Mark Appleton Thriller

CHAPTER ONE

JULY. TEHRAN, IRAN. IT wasn't just hot. It was hell. The heat
would melt shoes to the pavement if a person stood in one place
too long. The night air should bring some relief with its cool, musty
smell of sand and sweat. However, it seemed this evening the
cooling desert would not give up any of its pride and send a much-
needed breeze into the city. No, this night was muggy, sticky, and
just plain miserable.

Despite the heat, tonight was like any other night for Hokamend.
Seated on a pillow in his private quarters, he was reading, like he did
every night. This evening, the book was *The Fall of America*.

He and his best friend, who'd been killed in a bus bombing six
years earlier, had spent countless hours together going over the plans
and drawings of the Chicago metro system, trying to find the perfect
place to set off the explosive.

Muttering a prayer to Allah for success, he looked through the
open window at the sky and noticed it was devoid of stars. A storm
was moving in to tease them with the possibility of sweet relief from

the godforsaken heat. But he knew in the end the cloud would leave without so much as a drop of rain.

He envied his friend, who was in a place beyond this world, a place he could only dream of. He turned back to his book, reminding himself of all the work yet to be done. Someone had to complete the job, someone had to finish off those arrogant Americans.

His hatred for America and disdain for the people who infested the land made him want to spit. He pictured their smug faces and fancy cars. He would bring the infidels to their knees. He would wake the sleeping giant, then rip its head off.

A bodyguard walked past his door. He heard footsteps and it jolted him out of his daydream. His guards were the best that money could buy. They walked in four shifts and in different patterns every hour to keep lurking enemies confused. Hokamend was a careful man. He never took chances with his own life. True, he demanded his followers to give up their lives in service to Allah, but he was different. With a half-million-dollar American government bounty on his head, he was worth more, much more.

On the other hand, such a reward for betrayal could cause even friends to consider the offer. But he was no fool. Chopped off fingers, toes, and even a tongue now and then had a way of driving the truth home—under no circumstances should one cross Hokamend.

He slipped to his feet and walked to the double French doors leading out to a balcony, lighting up a cigar.

He touched the small scar above his right eye and smelled the cigar. "A battle wound," he would say. He was proud of his many scars. They proved his devotion to Allah. They proved he was not just an administrator but that he'd fought in the battles.

A small flicker flashed against the night sky as he struck the lighter and drew on his hand-rolled Cuban. He scanned his property, searching for snipers or anything that might be out of place but found nothing amiss, which didn't surprise him. After all, this was the perfect location for his palace. Situated at the apex of a hill, the mansion was surrounded by a high wall with guard towers at each corner manned by armed snipers. Beyond the wall, two chain-link fences made a wide circle around the perimeter of the grounds. Razor wire coiled across the tops of both fences, and fifteen highly trained guard dogs roamed in between. If someone were to make it past the first fence and was lucky enough to avoid the dogs, then the snipers would ensure he didn't see another sunrise.

An open lawn devoid of obstructions surrounded the palace in a one-mile circle. Deliberately designed so an enemy could not hide behind anything, the grounds looked more like a park than a secure compound.

He watched the city lights in the distance twinkle and blink like little bat eyes staring back at him, trying to ascertain if he was friend or foe. He took a deep draw, let out a cloud of thick smoke and wondered when they would figure it out, if ever. *No, they don't have the stomach for it. They are weak.*

A mosquito landed on his arm and started sucking blood like a miniature vampire. He swatted at the pest but missed as it dodged just in time to save its worthless life. "Stupid bugs," he muttered. They were out in force tonight, and there was no cool breeze to fend them off.

The mosquito buzzed by him again. He swung his hand at it and cursed. This time, he made contact with the bloodsucker, spreading a red smear across his arm.

He swore again. The nasty pests were ruining his quiet time. With his busy life, he treasured this hour of the day when he could think and clear his head, not to mention enjoy a good cigar.

He felt another prick on the side of his neck. More like a bee sting than a mosquito bite, this one hurt. He rubbed his neck but didn't feel anything unusual. In fact, he didn't feel anything. Nothing at all. His fingers were numb, like hard rubber chafing against his neck. A cold shiver ran up his spine. It was as if someone else was touching him. He had sensation in the rest of his body, but his hands were dead.

The bite began to throb, and a terrible heat burned through his body. He stumbled back into his study, drenched in sweat.

Screaming, he fell to the floor, clutching his head with unfeeling fingers. He dug his nails into his skull as if that would make the pain stop.

He yelled for a guard—anyone—to help him, but no one came to his aid.

The pain sharpened. His ears rang with a deafening sound like the air horns he'd heard as a boy just before a bomb exploded and more people died. Writhing on the floor, he shouted again for help. Then reality hit. No sound came out of his mouth. Just air.

Every nerve in his body flashed with impossible heat. Curled in a ball on the floor, he grasped his ears, trying to stop the noise that pounded against his skull.

Something was wrong with his ear. He pulled a hand away and blinked, not believing what he saw. Plastered in his palm, his right ear sizzled like a piece of hot bacon. He tried to focus, to make his brain work. But he couldn't think. The pain was beyond maddening. Mouthing a curse, he crushed the bloody ear in his hand as pain swept through his body like a wave of molten lava. The agony was so sharp and excruciating all he could do was writhe on the floor, clawing at his head and face.

Outside his door, his bodyguards took wagers as to which one he would curse tonight for not getting him his drink on time.

MARK APPLETON QUIETLY MADE his way down from his

rooftop perch, where he had just carried out another flawless hit. No one seemed to be aware of his presence, which was the way he liked it. Hokamend's guards wouldn't discover his body until the next morning. Most guards for hire these days were lazy alcoholics.

He'd hidden his blond hair under a dark baseball cap that matched the rest of his attire: black cargo pants, a long-sleeved black shirt with patches on the elbows and a tiny pocket on the left arm for his throwing knife, and black boots. His hands were covered in dark, lambskin gloves, which fit like a second skin. He silently slipped across the rooftop to a zip line, his access to this particular building.

Made of a small, woven cable used in airplane wings and developed by NASA, the eighth-inch line could support as much as three-thousand pounds. Using a high-powered yet small crossbow, he shot a tiny anchor at an adjacent building five hundred yards away. Once the anchor penetrated the brick it would spread to form a solid hold.

He slung his weapon over his shoulder, hooked himself to the line, and started his soundless descent to the shorter building. A door on the rooftop led to a back stairway. He crept through the abandoned building, which was empty except for a homeless drunk here and there. He wrinkled his nose. The smell of urine and mold made even the musty air outside seem like a fresh ocean breeze. He made sure he didn't wake any of the drunks as he traversed the twelve flights of stairs.

Once he was on the main level he made a right through a broken, wooden door into an empty room. Half of the wallpaper was torn off the walls and the carpet was long gone, leaving warped plywood behind. This part of town reminded him of tornado country. Some buildings were beautiful and untouched by the bombs. Others were about to cave in on themselves. War had a way of leaving its mark on more than just the people.

He quickly disassembled his weapon, and as he did so, searched the room for anything he might have left or any sign that could tie him to the dilapidated building. He folded the gun in half where the black barrel and plastic stock met. The scope snapped off with a soft click. His weapon of choice was custom made and could fire a paper round up to three miles, if the wind was right. He shoved the gun pieces in a backpack and hefted it onto his shoulder. Once everything was secure, he pulled a small remote from his pocket and stepped outside, where he peered around the corner, made sure no one spotted him, and pushed the button.

He could hear a faint sizzling sound as the zip line above him melted, then turned to ash and floated down in small flakes. Good, no trace. He ran across the street and walked three blocks south.

Tehran, like most cities in the desert, came alive after nightfall. People smoked outside the bars and griped about the heat. He could hear laughter from inside one bar he passed. Outside another he heard a thump, like someone falling off a chair, then the sound of glass shattering.

The streets were made of concrete and asphalt. Some intersections were lined with cobblestones. A multitude of blinking lights over storefronts strived to draw traffic to look at their wares. He made his way down a back alley, keeping his head down and avoiding eye contact. All he wanted was to get back to his place and get some sleep.

He stopped at a one-story shop with graffiti sprayed alongside the faded front door. A Persian sign above the door read *Sporting Goods*. The brick building wasn't much to look at with thick, black steel bars embedded in the wooden front door. The boarded-up windows also had the local kids' handiwork spray painted on them.

He inserted a key. The lock clicked. Using another key, he released the deadbolt. The heavy door creaked as he pushed it open and stepped inside. Pulling off his ball cap, he tossed it on the coat rack.

The shop was an open room with two rows of metal shelves in the middle stocked with a complete line of camping supplies: Coleman stoves and dehydrated foods ranging from stew to peach cobbler. Or for the old-school type, he could buy the original MREs and hope his taste buds were on vacation. The racks against the walls went all the way around the room and came to a stop at the front desk, which was topped by a cash register and a glass case containing pistols and knives. Behind the counter, guns of every shape and size, from shotguns to M16s, were racked from floor to ceiling. All of them had been previously owned but were in good working order.

The shop was not much, but it was clean, and it provided a good place for him to hide as he researched his target. The owner was a native who worked for the same organization he did. As far as anyone else was concerned, Mark was an out-of-town guest.

He stepped to the back of the little shop and stopped in front of a shelf full of books on how to fish and hunt and stay alive in the desert. He ran his fingers along the back of the books. When he located the fingertip-size button, he pushed it and a deep, groaning sound sliced the silence. The floor on his right split in the middle and opened up to reveal a concrete staircase. The hole was six-by-six and the concrete lid opened downward and hung like bomb bay doors on a plane. He started down and the floor closed above him with a solid thud. Wall lights flickered and came to life. At the bottom of the stairs, he stopped before a metal door with oversized rivets and bolts around the edges. A small, red light behind a glass bubble protruding from the wall glowed like an evil eye.

He placed his hand on the LCD screen mounted to the right of the door. The screen lit up and ran a scan of his handprint. He leaned down and spoke into a box, making sure to pronounce each syllable perfectly. "Appleton, Mark."

The red sensor above the door hummed as a red laser shot out and fanned at the end. Beginning at the top of his head, it scanned down his body, taking readings of his frame and measurements of each bone like an X-ray, though much more advanced. The light turned green when the scan was finished and the door unlocked and slid down into the floor.

What lay beyond was not a concrete bunker or a dingy underground hideout. Instead, it was a house. Not a real house, but it was as much of a house as one could get this far away from home. The first room looked like a typical American living room, minus the picture window. To the right was a kitchen with a black refrigerator, stove, and a microwave oven. To the left was a sitting area with a fireplace and a fifty-inch, surround-sound plasma screen television and a Blu-ray player. A couch with big, fluffy cushions faced the TV, and a camelhair rug graced the floor.

He punched a code on a keypad mounted on the wall on the far side of the living room, and a hidden door opened. The whooshing sound it made always reminded him of a Star Trek movie. Lights inside the room flashed on to reveal case after case of weapons and ammunition. He unpacked his backpack on a metal table that stood against a wall near the front of the weapons room. After he cleaned and oiled his gun, he placed it in an eight-foot glass case next to a Glock. Every wall supported similar cases containing guns, C4 explosives, landmines, and rocket launchers. Most of the weapons and ammo boasted his personal touches, from bullets made of paper to guns powered by air and sound waves.

At his touch the door whooshed back into place and blended into the wall as if it never existed. He stretched, pulled off his shirt, and ran his fingers through his hair. He craved a cool shower and a shave. The stakeout and events leading up to the kill had taken a year of stalking and many long, boring nights waiting for a clear shot.

The cool water felt good as it cascaded over his lean body and washed away the stress of the day.

He thought about the terrorist he'd just killed. He knew he should be sad or feel a little guilty about killing another man, but he couldn't bring himself to even feel bad. Because of all the things Hokamend had done—the bombings of schools and playgrounds that had killed and maimed dozens of children, and the snipers who shot twenty-plus people at a time in major American cities before anyone realized a massacre was in progress.

He turned off the water, thinking, *It's time for the terrorists of the world to live in fear instead of us fearing them.* After he shaved, he grabbed a pair of shorts from the dresser in his bedroom and slipped them on. Much better. Nothing like a comfortable pair of shorts.

In the kitchen, he pulled a dinner from the freezer and zapped it in the microwave. He turned the package over and saw that this dinner offered a tasty slab of chicken with mashed potatoes and a brownie to boot.

He chuckled. K certainly wouldn't approve. A microwave dinner and a soda? He could hear her exclaim, "Not healthy!" and see his wife's playful frown.

The smell of fake chicken filled the kitchen. He was too tired to cook tonight. Plus, he hadn't had a chance to restock his refrigerator. He sat down on the leather couch and began to eat.

Not bad, for a TV dinner. Not like K's cooking, though. Not much like anybody's cooking.

Now that he was on the subject, he couldn't help but think about K and his daughter, Samantha. It had been three years since…he shook his head, trying to shove the thought from his brain. *Wow. Three years. Time flies.*

Finished, he got up and threw the empty container in the trash, feeling a little celebratory. He was done with the mission and that meant only one thing.

Vacation—after a good night's sleep.

He turned off the lights and his alarm clock and crawled into his king-size bed. He was going to sleep in, which would be a nice change from the multiple all-nighters he'd pulled in the last year. He closed his eyes and drew the covers around his chin. No matter how hot it was outside, he had to be under the covers.

Once he had breathed in deep and let it all out in a long sigh, he relaxed his legs and arms. His eyes became heavy. Thoughts of his family consumed his mind until he fell asleep, which usually took a couple hours, but tonight he had a feeling he would fall asleep right away. He wished he could see K and her sparkling hazel eyes and the smile she reserved for him and him alone.

Then there was little Samantha, with her cute pigtails bobbing as she ran down the steps to meet him. The workday tensions melted when he felt her tiny arms hugging his neck. She always smelled like soap and lavender, no matter how dirty she was or how long she'd gone between baths. It seemed like just yesterday he was home holding K and Samantha in his arms. He hated to go to bed alone, again. So alone.

Three years earlier...

ABOUT THE AUTHOR:

AARON PATTERSON IS THE father of three kids: Soleil, Kale, and Klayton. He the New York Times and USA Today bestselling author of The Mark Appleton thriller series, The Airel Saga, and The Sarah Steele thriller series. He worked in the construction field for 11 years and is now a full time writer. He was home schooled and has a bachelor's degree in theology. He loves to hike, snowboard, camp, and drink coconut lattes. He is also the founder of StoneHouse Ink and co-founder of StoneHouse University. He speaks all over the country on the subjects of eBooks, writing and the changing publishing world.

Connect with Aaron at his blog: http://theworstbookever.blogspot.com

Friend him on Facebook: www.facebook.com/aaronpatterson

And follow him on Twitter: @mstersmith

Sign up for Aaron's newsletter for updates on his new books, and way cool deals including free eBooks. You will not get bugged with a ton of emails, you'll get a message only when he has something awesome to announce or give away.
Sign up here: http://eepurl.com/tQWHb